I0831503

AN OUTLAW'S JOURNAL

The following narrative depicts moments and characters based on historical events and people. Similarities with recorded fact are intentional, though artistic interpretation has been applied in these instances.

For more information go to: www.anoutlawsjournal.com/
To contact the author, email: anoutlawsjournal@gmail.com

First edition published in 2021

An Outlaw's Journal: Ah Nam
Stones, Georgina

ISBN 978-0-6453784-0-5
E-book ISBN 978-0-6453784-1-2

Formatted and edited by Aidan Phelan
Original illustrations by Aidan Phelan

Cover images:
Front - *The Chinese In Victoria. A Game Of Fan Tan.* The Illustrated Australian News, June 5, 1880. IAN05/06/80/85 [Courtesy: *State Library Victoria*]
Back - *Beechworth* by John William Lindt (ca. 1876), H42502/45 [Courtesy: *State Library Victoria*]

AN OUTLAW'S JOURNAL

Ah Nam

GEORGINA STONES

illustrated by Aidan Phelan

Australian Bushranging

Contents

Dedicated to

Joseph Byrne

Ellen Salisbury

Aaron Sherritt

As well as the Chinese of Beechworth and Sebastopol, in particular Ah Nam, and the girls of Little Bourke Street, Spring Creek.

And, of course, to my partner Aidan Phelan.

Prologue

Broken shards of terracotta and glass lie strewn across the floor of Ah Goon's gambling den in the Canton Camp at Spring Creek. The place has been alive with violence since the early hours of the morning, with a Chinese miner named Ah Nam being the cause of the ruckus. He resides in the Chinese camp in Sebastopol, but regularly travels between camps in the hope of finding fortune under the bark rooves of gambling dens. Unfortunately for the miner, his weakness for Fan-Tan had brought him into substantial debt and after he had refused to repay Ah Goon, Ah Nam was told he would no longer be welcome in his den until he paid his debts. This served as little more than a challenge for the tenacious miner and after he had spent the night in the passionate embrace of Ettie Noble, a prostitute he regularly visited at the brothel owned by Sarah Payne, he felt far above reproach. Ettie treated him with kindness and respect, something he certainly didn't receive from the European miners, and the pair's encounters were more than just a business transaction. He felt an affection for her, and just as his Chinese mates Ah Fee and Ah Tang had married white women, he hoped to one day make Ettie his bride.

With the light of daybreak filtering through the dusty shutters of the brothel, Ah Nam rises and walks groggily to the den of Ah Goon, where he is swiftly denied entry by the gambling den owner. Not allowing himself to be perturbed and still full of the wisdom only drink can offer, Ah Nam shrugs his shoulders and pretends to walk further up the lane. On reaching the cookhouse of Ye Man, he turns and looks back towards the gambling den, the aroma of chāsīu pork filling his nostrils as it wafts on the breeze. Seeing that Ah Goon has retreated back inside, Ah Nam follows his own slipper imprints back to the den and climbs in through an open window.

Standing shoulder to shoulder with the press of blurry eyed gamblers at the Fan-Tan table, it isn't long before the unwelcome gambler is spotted by Ah Goon. He rushes at him with the ferocity of a miner whose claim is being plundered, but Ah Nam doesn't move from his position and instead grabs a terracotta wine jug and smashes it over Ah Goon's head, leaving him bleeding and dripping with crimson coloured wine. In retaliation, the injured man picks up a shard from the broken pottery and slashes it across the base of Ah Nam's neck. He roars in pain and anger and falls back against the Fan-Tan table, upsetting the gamblers, who quickly join in the affray, with upturned furniture and smashed crockery soon scattered throughout the hut.

After a lull in the fighting, a bloodied Ah Goon is rushed to the Sun Quong Goon, the Chinese store owned by Nam Shing, while quietly Ah Nam curls himself on a piece of matting and beckons sleep.

I

After a morning spent herding his mother Margaret's milking cows with his brother Paddy, Joe Byrne, dressed in his town clothes and billycock hat, begins his journey up to Beechworth along the Woolshed Road, which is corrugated by recent rain. As is his usual wont, he has made sure to slip away while Margaret is in the dairy, finding it easier to leave quietly than to explain himself. His best mate Aaron Sherritt often mocks him for this, saying it's because Joe is frightened of his mother, but sixteen-year-old Joe just wishes for her to allow him to be who he is, and not merely what she wants him to be. Joe has no desire to be chained to life on the farm, he wants to savour all that is around him, but that has come at the cost of a fractured relationship between mother and son. It isn't fear that motivates him, but the pain of knowing how much more there is to life than cows and fences.

He glances upwards at the overhanging clouds, which again threaten rain, and hastens his pace past Thomas Lloyd's Eagle Hotel, where the Chinese cook, his queue braid wrapped around his head, kneels beneath the veranda scrubbing a cast iron pot. Up along the road in front of him, several European and Chinese miners argue close to Bishop's Shanty, one of the many that dot the Woolshed. One of the men, whose face and beard is blackened with soot, brandishes a pick, gesturing wildly to the Chinese miners. Joe steps aside as a hawker travels past and slows his pace. His father, also named Paddy, had always warned Joe not to stray within wielding distance, as the men were often mad with drink after a long day spent on their claim.

Adhering to this advice, Joe keeps his distance and walks out wide past the miners, with the three men sneering at him as he passes.

"You know where there's gold to be found don't you, eh?" the dumpy one of the trio sneers, swigging from a black bottle of gin.

Ignoring the taunt, Joe hears the rattle of wheels from behind him, as the Crawford & Co. coach rounds the bend, on route to El Dorado. He jumps out of the way as the four horse team canters past him, water splashing against the red painted sides

"Keep to the side, lad," the driver hollers, snapping the reins to urge the horses on before the climb.

***

Coming to the fork in the road at the foot of La Serena Hill, notorious for its steep incline and deep granite culvert running either side of it, Joe eyes the advertisement for Mr. Wright's drapery store, nailed to the trunk of a tree. He shakes his head at the sign, with its critical notice written in large black letters, "D. Wright has cheap drapery." A finger post, telling of which road to take to Beechworth would be more apt, as Joe himself concludes, but instead many storekeepers of the town had taken it upon themselves to mark these junctions with advertisements. A month ago, the *Ovens and Murray Advertiser* had published a letter to the editor which had been written by a visitor to Beechworth, who had gotten himself behind the bar of the Woolshed Inn twice, while trying to find the correct road leading to Beechworth. Joe had found the gentleman's plight amusing, owing largely to the fact that on several occasions he had been hailed down by a flustered newcomer to Beechworth, who had turned off the road too quickly and looped back to Sebastopol.

***

Arriving in Beechworth, Joe walks past the imposing granite walls of Beechworth Gaol and rounds the corner of Ford Street towards the government camp.

Nearing the courthouse, he hears the cries for leniency from inside, before the resounding thud of the hammer silences the building. The heavy wooden door is pulled open and a boy, dressed in rags, is hauled outside by a police sergeant.

"The next time you cause such disruption, you'll find yourself acquainted with the lockup," the heavy set man barks, pushing the lad onto the footpath.

Joe steadies his pace to watch, while the agitated boy fumbles with his hat and pulls it over his matted blonde hair.

"Old Stewart is innocent," he yells, kicking crushed granite up at the officer. "He never broke into Mrs. Devlin's house in Finch Street, you've locked up the wrong man!"

The sergeant's face glows red with rage at being spoken to with such insolence. He brandishes a pair of handcuffs and jangles them threateningly

"I'm allowing you a chance to leave quietly, boy. If you do not care for your liberty, I will be compelled to arrest you!"

"You've already taken one man's liberty, what difference will mine make?" the boy retorts sarcastically and scoops up a fistful of crushed granite, throwing it in the uniformed man's face.

Cursing loudly, the injured man doubles over and clutches a hand over his eye. He blows hard on his whistle as the boy runs across the road towards the Albion Hotel.

"Where the hell are you, Mullane?" he bellows, blowing on the metal mouth piece again.

Alerted by the high-pitched whistle, a constable emerges from the police yard, Joe's eyes fixing on his spurs which glint in the sunlight.

"Smith's bastard of a son..." the sergeant wheezes, still clutching his right eye, "...dressed in rags; headed up Ford Street!"

The constable stands, unmoving, a look of confusion spread across his face.

"What are you looking at, you fool?" the sergeant snaps, "get after him!"

"Yes sir," he replies with a salute, before sprinting up Ford Street in pursuit of the boy.

The sergeant turns, irritated, to Joe and the small collection of bystanders that have gathered around the courthouse.

"You've all had your entertainment, now get on your way!"

***

Coming to the crossroads of Ford and Camp Street, Joe looks towards the Hibernian Hotel, recognising the familiar figures of Aaron Sherritt and James Wallace as they stand beneath the hotel's veranda. With Aaron dressed in his usual mismatch of clothing, the ensemble finished with a bright red sash tied around his waist.

"Oi, Byrne," he shouts at the top of his voice, causing the couple stepping out of the Bank of New South Wales to stare in bewilderment at the flash-dressed seventeen-year-old, as he swaggers toward Joe, with a pie from Dunlop's in his hand.

Waiting for a buggy to pass, Aaron and James cross the road.

"Good to see you James," Joe says, holding out his hand.

James shakes it weakly and smiles unconvincingly, his eyes crinkling at their corners.

"You too, Joe."

Joe had known James since a mere boy, with the pair of them sitting together during their lessons at the Woolshed Catholic School.

"You managed to get away from the old woman, then?" Aaron asks, taking a bite of the pastry.

"I didn't tell her I was leaving. After Paddy and I had finished milking, I got dressed and left. Besides, I'm only intending on being in town for a couple of hours. She'll hardly notice my absence."

Aaron nods cheekily and elbows James in the ribs.

"I suppose it won't be any different to the last time she 'hardly noticed' you were gone."

Joe shakes his head and looks away, knowing too well what Aaron has left to say.

"Only she did notice, didn't she Joe?" Aaron asks rhetorically, his mouth twisted in a smirk. "And she took to you with the bloody broom!"

Joe's face burns crimson at the memory of his mother swatting him like a fly with the broom. The rough straw that stung across his forearms like the rap of the cane across his knuckles, issued by Mr. O'Donoghue when his attention was taken during his lessons.

Pushing the memory to the back of his mind, he gestures towards James Ingram's bookshop. A favoured hideaway.

"I'm planning on going to Ingram's to read. What have you both come to town for?"

Aaron conveys the remaining bit of pie into his mouth, splodges of gravy dripping onto his fingers.

"Ingram's?" he drawls, wiping his hands across his moleskins. "Come to the Burke Museum with me and James, you can waste your time reading any day of the week."

***

On entering the museum, Joe and James remove their hats, with the trio soon greeted by a stout, suited man in spectacles, his thinning hair slicked back against his scalp, called Mr. Arundel. Tapping a rod against a mounted signboard, he proceeds to address them of the rules, all the while paying particular attention to the way Aaron is dressed, who, as Joe himself notes, appears as if he is an agent for Ashton's Circus.

With his lecture concluded, the gentleman turns to Aaron, an air of haughtiness spread across his countenance.

"Sir, is there a particular reason why you have kept your hat on?"

Aaron glances at the hat rack, where hats of varying sizes and descriptions are hanging.

Muttering beneath his breath, Aaron removes his hat and defiantly tucks it under his arm.

Walking past the rows of long wooden writing desks that Joe would normally be sitting at and reading, he follows Aaron and James through to the display of taxidermy. The floor boards creak beneath their boots and Joe does his best to shift the weight to his toes, knowing too well the disapproving looks one is liable to receive if they disturb the readers. They file past the Maltby globe and stand before the glass cabinets which display the museum's collection of taxidermied king parrots, eagles, lyrebirds, bitterns and owls.

With his attention taken by a marble bust of Queen Victoria, Aaron steps back against the display case, causing it to rock momentarily.

Mr. Arundel rises swiftly from his desk, an expression of frustration etched across his face.

"Would you mind keeping your distance from the displays, sir?"

Joe glares at Aaron.

"Watch where you're going, you fool."

"It's not my fault there's hardly any room here," Aaron replies, his voice a sharp whisper.

"Just bloody watch where you're going," Joe says, feeling embarrassed by his mate's idiocy.

Aaron shrugs off the instruction and tips his head toward Mr. Arundel, who watches the trio over the rim of his spectacles.

"Did you see how quickly the old bugger sprung up from his chair?"

James laughs into the lapel of his coat, in an attempt to muffle his amusement.

"Like one of those jack-in-the-boxes," he chuckles, as he views a white ibis through the pane of glass, the bird's feathers covered in a grey layer of dust.

Joe leaves the pair and moves through to the adjoining room, where a collection of Aboriginal weapons is displayed. He examines the array of spears, shields and boomerangs with interest, marvelling at the craftsmanship and detail of each object. Continuing through the room, Joe's eyes rest on a twisted pair of South African antelope horns, adorned on brass hooks. Puzzled by their use, he reads the labelled description, indicating the horns are used for music.

From the next room, Aaron's heavy footsteps can be heard as he moves about the exhibition.

He pokes his head around the corner, "Joe," he calls, "come and look at this!"

An elderly gentleman who stands stooped at a table, looks up indignantly from the collection of gemstones he is studying.

"Young man, you are in a museum, not a public house."

Aaron's eyes drop to the brightly coloured stones that are lined in rows along the table. He has seen many of their like before, shimmering beneath the water of Reedy Creek.

"Aren't people allowed to talk in museums?" he asks, glancing up at the gentleman.

"Not at the top at their voices."

"Are you in charge of the place?"

"You do not need to be 'in charge' to adhere to public etiquette," the gentleman answers.

Aaron scowls at the address.

"And they teach that at the Benevolent Asylum, do they?"

James looks towards Joe with a frown, "Will he ever learn to stop playing the fool?"

Aaron swaggers back towards them.

"Bugger this place, let's go up Ford Street," he announces, putting his hat on and pulling the strap under his bottom lip.

Joe sighs at the order and removes his father's watch from his pocket. Holding it in his palm he looks forlornly at the hands.

"It's already eleven thirty."

"So?" Aaron shrugs, "What does the time have to do with our leaving?"

"If I am to read at Ingram's and make it home before dusk, I don't have time to be strolling up and down Ford Street."

Aaron shakes his head and claps his hand on Joe's back, as if he directing a sheep through a race.

"Lighten up would you, there'll be time for your precious books."

Knowing he is left with no other choice, Joe follows Aaron and James back onto Loch Street.

***

The trio walk beneath the verandaed shop fronts, stopping to peer in at the window displays, each more decoratively furnished than the previous one. Coming to Daniel McNamara's saddlery, Joe cups his hands to the glass and gazes through the pane at a well-oiled saddle that sits on a wooden stand. The well-crafted piece of tack is nothing like the saddle he rides in, with its cracked pommel and oil stain from where his younger brother, Denny, had mindlessly left an oily rag lying across it.

His eyes wander to the opposite wall, where rows of harnesses hang from metal hooks. Seeing Joe peering through the glass, Daniel raises his arm from the work bench he sits at, punching holes into a strip of leather.

"It's a good one. Pigskin and all," he declares, gesturing with the leather punch. "It'll help you to stick superbly to any horse."

Joe nods at the claim and glances back at the saddle, wishing he had the money to purchase it. However, his daydream is quickly aborted by the persistent nudging of Aaron.

"Here, Joe, isn't that Jim Tatham?"

Joe turns and looks across the street at Greer's grocer, where a young man conveys a crate of pears onto a table.

"I think so."

Aaron narrows his eyes at the grocer's assistant.

"I haven't seen the bugger for almost a year."

With his attention taken, Aaron swaggers to the edge of the footpath; the swift action causes him to almost collide with a man carrying a bag of Tomlin's flour.

"James," he yells, unruffled by the scowl he receives from the flour carrying gent.

Thinking he is the James that Aaron is calling to, James Wallace turns from the Wellington boots in John Carew's window.

"What is it?"

Aaron waves a hand to dismiss his question and repeats his call to Jim Tatham.

"Oi, Tatham!"

With the last of the pears arranged, Jim studies the street and raises his arm in greeting at the sight of Aaron and Joe.

"Come on," Aaron says, glancing over his shoulder at Joe and James Wallace.

Crossing the street, Joe and James follow Aaron to Greer's, where Jim stands beneath the shop's veranda, the empty pear crate resting against his shin.

Joe shakes his hand.

"What are you three fellows doing in town?" Jim asks, glancing hesitantly in the doorway for the presence of his boss, William Greer.

"Well, me and Wallace are going for a drink at the Harp of Erin. I can't speak for Joe, though. Reckons he's going to waste the day reading in Ingram's dingy back room."

Joe scowls at the remark and steps back as a stray Collie dog sniffs at his bluchers.

"Books are liquor for the mind, aren't they Joe?" Jim asks with a wink.

Joe nods, acknowledging Aaron's confused expression with a laugh.

"I wouldn't expect you to understand that, Aaron," Joe says cheekily, running a hand through the dog's matted fur.

Aaron shoots Joe a wounded expression. For all his larrikin whim, he had always been self-conscious about the intellectual divide that existed between himself and Joe.

"Go back to your precious books, then."

"Aye, I will," Joe replies, with a tip of his hat.

***

Having finally made it to James Ingram's bookshop, Joe sits in the cluttered back room, reading *The Count of Monte Cristo*, a novel most favoured by him since Mr. O'Donoghue had first suggested it to him five years previously. From behind the curtained doorway, James Ingram's voice echoes as the Scotsman directs a female customer on what seeds are best planted during the cooler autumn months.

Picking up the small teapot, Joe pours himself a cup of black tea and drops a sugar cube into the steaming liquid. Whenever Joe visits Ingram's shop, he is always given time to browse the shelves and select a book to read in the back room, with the Scotsman keeping it aside for him until he next visits. Joe relishes the opportunity to read undisturbed and to allow himself to become immersed in the story. Finding the peace to read with such immersion at Sebastopol is often a hard task, with his younger siblings never far. At the times when he seeks solace in the gully, or at the falls, Aaron soon follows him, and it isn't long before an argument erupts over Aaron's noisy attempts to grab his attention.

Joe sips the tea and looks across at the endless abundance of stock, piled high against the walls. A thick layer of dust covers the cases, which are full of children's toys and books. When Joe had first been ushered into the storeroom, after James had found him reading *Oliver Twist* amongst the shelves, he couldn't quite believe his eyes. Never had he seen such an array.

Bringing his attention back to the pages of *The Count of Monte Cristo*, the bustle of the street resounds as the shop door is opened once again.

"Good afternoon Mr. Shing," James greets the Chinese storekeeper, "how be yer health on this pleasant afternoon?"

"And a good afternoon to you too, Mr. Ingram," Nam Shing replies in his familiar tone, "it is indeed a very nice day. Much more pleasant now that the rain has left us."

"Now that much is certain," Ingram remarks assuredly, "for a few days there I was thinking I'd be needing tae replace my roof. I've ne'er seen so much water spilling from my gutters."

Joe smiles to himself as he turns the page of his book, Ingram had been frantic with worry about his roof and the need to replace it, which had very much annoyed the bootmaker next door, whose shop was under the adjoining roof.

"The Canton Camp has been truly terrible," Nam Shing remarks, "muddy enough for lotus flowers to grow."

"I suppose that will have put a halt on yer rebuilding efforts?"

"Only slightly. I am much obliged to my countrymen; they are willing to work in all conditions."

A month before, a fire had broken out in Ah Chee's hut and quickly spread to the neighbouring structures. The lottery shop, Nam Shing's residence and huts belonging to Ah Ho, Tu Lip, Yu Men, Ah Gee, Ah Tak and Yu Men were also lost in the blaze. The fire had started in the wood carter's hut by the supposed carelessness of Ah Chee's housekeeper, who had replaced keeping an eye over the fire with gossiping on the street, or at least that is how the *Ovens and Murray Advertiser* had reported the incident. The ferocity of the fire was quickly made known throughout the district, with the smoke and stench covering much of Beechworth.

"Well, I am glad tae hear it," Ingram responds, "what is it I can be doing for ye, Mr. Shing?"

"I am needing your advice Mr. Ingram. Ah Nam is causing much disturbance and I need to get him back to Sebastopol, but I have not found anyone I can trust willing to take him back that way."

James Ingram is seen by many as the guardian of the camp and had recently stepped in when a group of boys attempted to stir up the quiet Chinese. As a sign of their gratitude, some members of the Canton Camp had gifted the bookseller with jars of preserved ginger and fresh vegetables from their gardens.

"Hmm," the Scotsman ponders, "I have young Joseph Byrne reading in my storeroom, I believe he'll be journeying back tae Sebastopol sometime soon."

"I know the young man well. He is most respectful and speaks our language well."

"Joseph," Ingram calls, "Mr. Shing is here tae see ye."

Joe puts the book down and stands, straightening the creases out of his trousers.

Emerging from the curtain, he sees the wealthy Chinese shopkeeper, his crow-black hair cropped short, wearing his favourite tweed suit with a polished gold watch chain hanging from his silk waistcoat. James Ingram stands beside him, dressed in a long black coat and cravat, an encyclopedia under each arm.

Nam Shing greets Joe with a bow, "Néih Hóu, Ah Joe. I'm glad to find you looking well."

"Néih Hóu," Joe bows, "thank you."

"I have a proposition for you, if you would be gracious enough to accept it? I have been sent word that Ah Nam is causing trouble in the camp. He has been gambling at Ah Goon's in Little Bourke Street and has not repaid the debts owed. I am requiring him to be collected from that place and taken back to Sebastopol."

"M̀haih", Joe replies with a shake of his head. "Ma won't be happy if I'm late home."

Nam Shing dismisses Joe's concern with a wave of his hand.

"What if I offered you a pound for your service?"

"Surely ye won't be begrudging a pound, lad?" James Ingram interjects, nodding toward the one-pound bank note Nam Shing holds in his fingers.

Joe hesitates for a moment, the look of disappointment on his mother's face etched into his mind. He shakes his head.

"M̀haih, no. Ma will have me in the stable if I am late."

"Would you be persuaded if I wrote a note to your mother, explaining your absence?"

Feeling the weight of responsibility on his shoulders, Joe concedes with a nod of his head. Nam Shing smiles.

"A pencil and piece of paper, please Mr. Ingram."

"Aye, of course," replies James, turning to rummage through the top draw of his counter.

"Here ye go, Mr. Shing."

Nam Shing takes them from him with a bow of his head and begins writing his note, the pressure of his grasp on the pencil causing it to audibly scrape across the wooden surface of the counter. The note completed; he hands it to Joe.

"There should be no problem for you now, Ah Joe."

Joe's eyes flick over the elaborate handwriting.

'Mrs. Byrne,

The absence of your son Joseph is on my account and mine alone. I have asked him to accompany Ah Nam home to his hut at the Sebastopol Chinese camp. I do not trust anyone else with the task. Please forgive his delay.

Yours faithfully,

Mr. William Nam Shing of Spring Creek, Beechworth.'

"Dòjeh," Joe answers in gratitude, tucking the note into his pocket.

"I believe Ah Nam is an acquaintance of yours?"

"Yes, I am acquainted with him. He lives in a hut with Ah Fook and Ah Kee."

"Ah Kee," Nam Shing smiles, "I have not seen him for many years. How is his health?"

Visions of the sickly miner begin to swirl in Joe's mind, Ah Kee had once been a jovial member of the Sebastopol camp, his sluice box blessing him with much good fortune. But his health had suffered greatly in the past few months, and despite the urging of his fellow miners, Ah Kee wouldn't consult the doctor, believing them to be the bringers of bad luck and death.

"He doesn't leave his hut often," Joe begins, "and when he does, he is always supported either side. I am surprised he has not sought your help."

Nam Shing looks downcast.

"My help has been offered to him and on many occasions..." he trails off and waves a hand as if to dispel the concern. "Bá paau," he says making a fist on his chest, "he is a foolish man with too much pride."

II

After finishing the scalding cup of black tea James had insisted upon him having before he left, Joe steps out with the storekeeper, his gold watch reflecting in the window of Young's Boot Store as they walk down Camp Street toward the Spring Creek camp.

"Thank you for accepting to take Ah Nam back to Sebastopol. I do not trust my people with the task, the man is a trickster and will pretend he is ill. I hope to never see him return."

"I'm glad to help," Joe lies, feeling anxious at being the one to persuade Ah Nam to leave Ah Goon's gambling house.

While he knows the man on friendly terms, Joe is also acutely aware of how unpredictable the miner's mood can be. In February, Ah Nam had returned back to his hut rattled with drink and hunger. On seeing no rice in the cooking pot, he had quarrelled violently with Ah Fook, even going so far as to attempt to throw the man into the fire. The news of this attack had spread rapidly through the camp, with Joe hearing the tale from Aaron's brother Jack Sherritt, who shared a gold claim with the near burnt man.

Shaking the memory from his mind, he and Nam Shing pass the Empire Hotel, where the loud chatter of drinkers and card players flows from the open doors. Joe glances into the window, recognising one of the drinkers as John Phelan, the local dog catcher and pound keeper, who

Aaron has started breaking in horses for. Despite his mate's protests that he was alright, Joe found Phelan to be an unlikeable rogue, who had no qualms with using the friendship of others for his own benefit.

Turning down the lane of Little Bourke Street, two flash-dressed women stand either side of a table, where a group of Chinese men gamble what money they have. The veranda of the hut is animated by the squawking sulphur-crested cockatoos that bob up and down in their cages. As they pass the men, one of them, his face a mess of pockmarks, looks up and tips his head. Little Bourke Street is notorious for its brothels, gambling dens and the women who call it home, with the *Ovens and Murray Advertiser* taking great pleasure in detailing the depravity that is conducted in this area. But, as Joe himself noted, there was never any reporting of the dancing girls who frequented several of the hotels in Beechworth, or the drunks who would fall into the gutters and stay there snoring till morning.

Continuing down the lane, the infamous madam of the Chinese Camp, Sarah Payne, stands beneath the veranda of her notorious residence, an ornate fan fluttering in her fingers. She steps aside as a Chinese miner stumbles out of the doorway, tucking his tunic into his rough woollen trousers.

"I hope to be seeing you again soon, sweetheart," she says, her lips parting in a sly grin.

The miner acknowledges her with a nod of his head, and he tosses her a small bag of coins, before disappearing into the darkness of an opium den.

Sarah is joined under the veranda by a younger woman in a lilac-coloured dress with a tightly cinched waist, her soft face framed by a mess of auburn curls. Joe looks across at the girl, his eyes settling on the open buttons of her bodice and chemise, revealing the milky white skin of her chest.

Sarah winks and motions with a slender finger for him to enter. "Plenty of girls for a sweetheart like you," she offers.

Noticing Joe looking at her, the young woman brushes open the fabric provocatively, exposing the roundness of her breasts and lifts her skirts. His mouth falling open as his eyes lock on the exposed skin.

"No need to be shy," Sarah continues, "you'll find Brigid is most obliging. Especially for such a handsome young man."

Feeling himself enticed, Joe goes to step forward but Nam Shing pulls him away.

"Joseph, this is most certainly not a place for respectable gentlemen," he says sternly, turning back to the two women, "have you no common decency?"

Feigning offence, Sarah clutches her chest, "No common decency, sir?"

"Yes, that is what I said," Nam Shing confirms, "no person of decency would act so wantonly in a public street."

"A thousand pardons, sir," she answers sarcastically, "but when a lad shows interest, myself and Brigid here are going to offer. How else do you expect us to survive? Begging on the street?"

"There is little difference that I can see," he remarks, looking on the woman with disdain, "you should be ashamed of your actions."

Sarah snaps her fan shut and steps toward Nam Shing, coming eye to eye with the storekeeper.

"It might not be to your taste mister, but my customers are well pleased for the service. Besides, do you think your practice of replacing Hennessy brandy with cheaper stuff, is not commonly known? You and your kind are hypocrites."

Joe attempts to hide his smile, but the upward curling of his lips give him away, while Nam Shing fumes at the woman's audacity.

Seeing the storekeeper has nothing left to say, Sarah winks at Joe and turns toward the door, exaggerating the movement of her hips as she moves inside.

***

On their arrival to the gambling house, the dark clouds that have been threatening rain finally succumb and it falls in heavy sheets over Beechworth. Joe and Nam Shing seek refuge under Ah Goon's bark veranda, the brightly coloured banners snapping back and forward with the wind. A large tabby cat that had been stalking a mouse beside the drain suddenly scampers to join them and scratches its claws against the veranda post.

Nam Shing looks on the hut with disdain and wipes away the droplets that cling to his forehead.

"This is where I leave you Joseph," Nam Shing begins, "for if I have to be in the same room as the wretched man, I fear I might kill him."

Joe accepts the explanation with a nod and cautiously enters the darkened gambling house. He glances around the squalid room, where signs of fighting are evident in a mess of shattered pottery and upturned furniture. A group of Chinese men recline to the left of him in an opium induced stupor, their long bamboo pipes cradled possessively in their arms.

The unmistakable rumble of snoring catches his attention and he hesitantly steps forward, the shards of glass crunching beneath his bluchers like thick alpine snow. Below a shelf of unscathed ceramic mijiu bottles, Ah Nam lies sleeping on a piece of matting.

Crouching down, Joe whispers sharply in the sleeping man's ear.

"Ah Nam, get yourself up."

The dozing miner swats him away with the back of his hand.

"M̀h'hóu dihm ngóh," he snarls, warning Joe not to touch him.

"Get up," Joe repeats, unintimidated, "it's me, Ah Joe."

Ah Nam rubs at his eyes and focuses his gaze on Joe, a look of surprise covering his sleep lined face.

"Ah Joe," he mumbles, sitting up, "I not know it was you. Hóunoih móuhgin."

"I'm here to take you back to Sebastopol, William Nam Shing sent me."

Ah Nam looks at Joe confused.

"Néih góng mātyéh wá?"

"You owe money. Mē jaa," Joe asserts.

"Ah Goon?"

Joe raises an eyebrow.

"What about Ah Goon?"

"He was one who squealed like pig?"

"He said you would not repay the debts owed."

"Huh?" Ah Nam frowns, itching at the bloodied scars on his neck, "Tùhng ngóh góng gwóngdùngwá."

Joe takes out his coin purse and shakes it to make his meaning clearer.

"You not pay Ah Goon, that is why you need to return to Sebastopol. You have no choice."

"Gām'yaht?"

"Haih, gām'yaht. He wants you out of the camp today."

Ah Nam laughs sharply at the accusation and rubs a finger across the black stains of his teeth.

"Wāisigéi," he grunts, pointing towards a chipped terracotta jug on the table.

Joe follows his direction and picks up the jug, his nose wrinkling at the harsh vapour of cheap grog.

"Whiskey?"

"Whis-key," Ah Nam echoes, "Haih."

Snatching the vessel from him, the miner takes a large swig, causing an excess of liquor to run down his neck and glaze the open wounds. Joe averts his eyes as Ah Nam's face creases into a grimace, knowing the outburst that will soon follow.

"Diu!" He curses in pain, throwing the jug against the slab wall.

***

Having finally persuaded Ah Nam to leave the gambling den, the two begin walking up the muddy lane towards Sarah Payne's brothel. A feeling of reluctance fills Joe at the thought of having to pass the building again, after the flustered state Brigid had left him in only an hour before.

"I not go until I see Ettie," Ah Nam declares, pointing a bloodied hand towards the brothel.

Joe's brow furrows at the demand.

"Ettie?"

"Haih. She my girl. I not go back until I tell her goodbye."

"We haven't the time," Joe utters nervously.

Ah Nam dismisses him and walks towards the brothel. On his approach, a young woman dressed in little more than combination undergarments, runs towards Ah Nam.

"My love," Ettie giggles, throwing her arms around Ah Nam's neck.

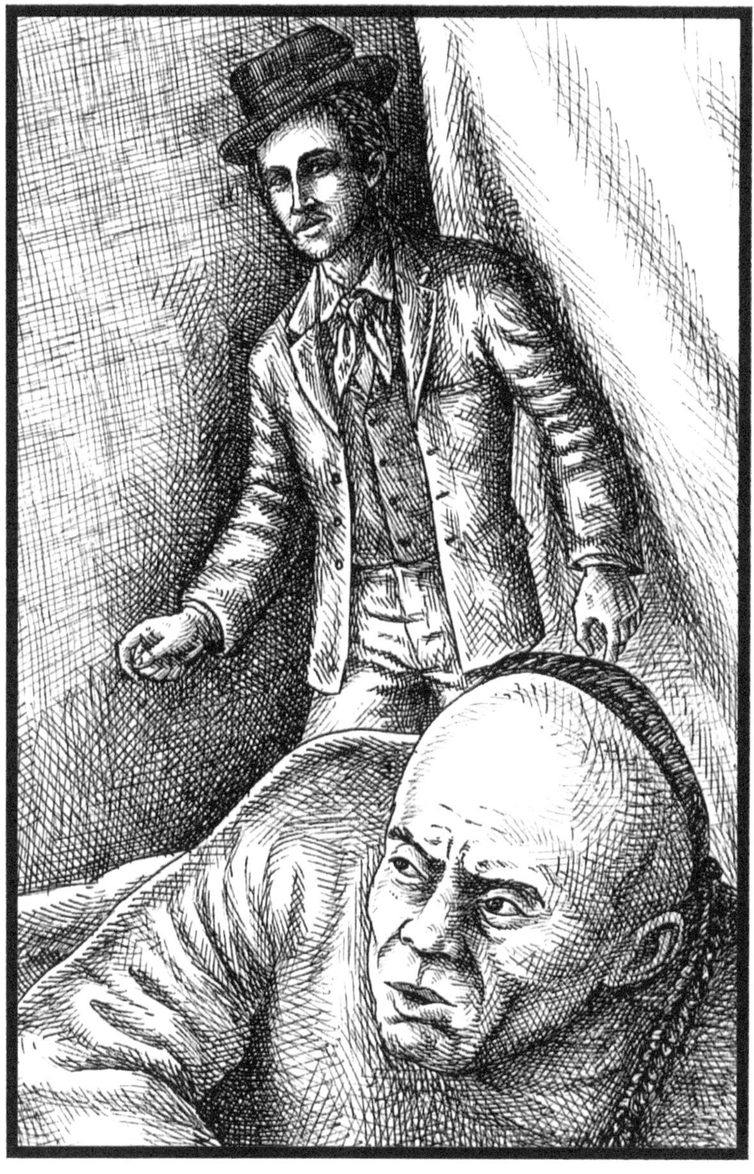

Ah Nam's expression softens like butter in a hot pan and the pair share a passionate kiss, mingled with giggling from Ettie, as her lover pinches her backside. She pulls back and runs her fingers over the glistening cuts on his face and neck.

"What happened here?" she asks.

"Ah Goon not let me play Fan-Tan. He tell me to leave, but I not go without fight,"

Ettie strokes Ah Nam's forehead.

"You know you shouldn't stir Ah Goon's anger in that way."

He addresses her concern with a wad of spit directed at the ground.

"His anger not like mine."

She rolls her eyes at his show of bluster and turns her attention to Joe.

"Who might your handsome friend be?" Ettie enquires, her dark eyes examining Joe with temptation.

"My name's Joseph Byrne, ma'am," he says, noticing the raised scar that runs down her cheek.

"Are you here for Brigid, Joseph Byrne? I saw you through the window earlier with Nam Shing. She hoped you might be coming back."

As if on cue, Brigid emerges from the darkened doorway of the brothel and walks toward Joe, the frayed hem of her skirt sweeping over the dampened earth.

"You came back," she says, her voice a soft purr.

Joe smiles, feeling himself trembling beneath the expression of desire that is cast across her face.

"I'm really very accommodating," she attests, running a slender finger down his waistcoat to the waistband of his tweed trousers.

The action causes Joe to shiver, the sensation pulsing through him like nothing he has ever experienced before. Bridget acknowledges his nervousness with a kiss on his cheek, her lips warm against his skin. Placing her hands around his chin, Bridget lowers Joe's head to hers and kisses him passionately, her mouth tasting sweet with the flavours of opium smoke and gin. Peeling herself away, she tugs on his hand to lead him inside. Impulsively, Joe follows but as they near the doorway, he stops and let's go of Brigid's hand.

"No, I can't," he says, his mind burdened with a sense of responsibility. "I am here to take Ah Nam back to Sebastopol for Nam Shing."

Bridgid pouts her lips sulkily

"I promise I will make it worth your while."

Joe blushes at the statement and shakes his head. No matter the thrill that might be offered inside those slab walls, he knows the promises he has made cannot be ignored.

"Ah Nam," Joe says abruptly, turning his back on Brigid, "we're going now."

***

Walking past the Vine Hotel on Sydney Road, the melodic tune of a piano plays from within, while a woman's voice sings in synchronisation with the music.

Ah Nam rolls his sleeves up past his elbows, exposing the protruding veins of his forearm.

"Ngóh séung yiu sāang'gwó," he says, pointing to the overhanging branches of Jacob Vandenberg's apple tree.

Joe shrugs at the request. Scrumping for apples had never been a point of contention for him, with he and Aaron often making raids on Anton Wick's apple and pear trees in the Woolshed. Once spying the pair, the German would yell at them in his thick accent, like an angry farmer yelling at crows who greedily peck his seeds. His reprimands did little to discourage the pair, and it became more of a challenge than anything else.

"Take one if you wish."

Ah Nam reaches up and grabs an apple, biting nosily into the ripe flesh.

"Ah Goon is dog," he announces with a mouth full of half chewed apple, "he be sorry. I'll make him sorry."

Joe sighs at the vitriol and shakes his head. His travelling companion's constant complaints and promises for vengeance is wearing thin. Why couldn't Aaron or James Wallace have been tasked with conveying Ah Nam home? Why does everything seem to fall around his shoulders, like a heavy wooden yoke? Keeping the feeling of resentment locked deep within, Joe looks down toward the valley, where he knows his mother would be uttering every oath at his absence.

"Let's just concentrate on getting back to Sebastopol before the moon is in the sky," he asserts finally.

III

As Joe and Ah Nam make their way along the Woolshed Road, the miners who Joe had passed on his way up to Beechworth, still loiter outside Bishop's shanty, their laboured movements a testament to the amount of alcohol they had consumed.

"You brought a yellow bastard back with you, eh?" one of them calls, issuing a bout of crude laughter from the others.

Ah Nam stops still and turns toward the men.

"Chíngmahn dím chīngfū? What I call you?" he retorts.

"They're stupid with drink Ah Nam," Joe urges, understanding the threat, "they don't know what they are saying."

"Wòhng sīk?" Ah Nam asks the men, ignoring Joe's urging.

The fatter of the three steps forward and gestures a profanity with his sausage-like fingers.

"You ain't in China now. Speak English you dirty ching."

Ah Nam's face contorts into a grimace.

"Ching?"

The miner glares down on him mockingly.

"That's the word for little fellas like you."

Ah Nam tips his head back, a wad of spit forming in his mouth.

"Don't you dare!" The man begins, his voice trailing off in a splutter when a covering of phlegm lands in his grimy beard.

"You yellow bastard," he roars, smashing the gin bottle against the stump.

Joe attempts to restrain Ah Nam, but he breaks free and hurls his five-foot-three frame towards the brute, clutching his hands around his neck. The pair grapple violently as Ah Nam attempts to strangle the crimson faced miner, who gasps and curses against the tightening grip. Wary of the man's mates, Joe attempts to pull Ah Nam away, but the two men merely watch on, stunned with drink, like bullocks dealt a blunt blow.

Finally seeing his chance, Joe clutches his hand around Ah Nam's tunic and tears him away. The nearly-strangled miner falls heavily to the ground, gasping like a fish taken from water. Seeing his aggressor lying helpless, Ah Nam removes his slipper and commences to hit the miner across the face. With his attention taken on again subduing Ah Nam, Joe is unaware of the second miner who lurches at him from behind, a look of murderous impulse plastered on his weathered face. The man grasps the collar of Joe's sack coat and pulls him backwards, landing him on the ground. He brandishes a pick high above his head with a growl. Knowing he is a dead man if he doesn't move quick, Joe jumps to his feet and ducks from the man's drunken swings. A bout of anger pulses through him and he wraps his arms around the miner's mid-section and throws him into the mud. The crowd that has formed around them jeer at the spectacle; their wild expressions hungry for blood.

Keenly aware that the growing number might attract the interest of the local constable, Joe shoves his hands into Ah Nam's back to move him forward, as if driving on a stubborn horse.

"Gòu le!" Joe shouts angrily, "That's enough!"

***

With the madness of earlier still painted on Ah Nam's face, the pair cross the footbridge over Reedy Creek. Joe glances down between the wooden planks at the murky water that swells in a torrent, while inside his head his thoughts are doing the same. With each step toward

Sebastopol the harshness of his mother's words grows louder, and no matter how hard he tries to shake them her disappointment is inescapable. He slips a hand into his pocket and fingers the note Nam Shing has written explaining his absence, hoping it will not have been all for nothing.

Ah Nam glances at Joe's apprehensive expression with a frown.

"Ah Joe?"

Joe takes in the darkening sky with a shake of his head; he should have been home hours ago.

***

Trudging along the road, Joe's eyes follow the muddy tracks made by a wagon, the ache of his legs making him wish he was the one riding in it. As they pass Abraham's store, the cursing of a young man can be heard up ahead.

Joe glances toward Ah Nam, whose lip twitches in agitation as the stationary wagon comes into view, with two girls and a boy sitting beside the conveyance on the roadside. Anxious of Ah Nam, Joe goes to give the trio a wide berth, but something tells him that they need help.

On their approach, the younger of the two girls look nervously at Joe and Ah Nam, her arms tightening around her chest. Aware of her reaction, Joe removes his hat and offers her a smile.

"My name is Joseph Byrne," he says politely, "I see you've encountered some trouble."

She nods silently, drawing her knees up to her chest.

"We lost a piece of iron from the harness."

Joe studies the girl's face, her features suddenly familiar to him.

"You're James Salisbury's daughter, aren't you? I remember seeing you outside the Oriental Hotel after the inquest on Ah Suey."

"How do you know my father?"

"He was one of me and my father's regular customer's when we were hawking firewood. I remember seeing you hanging washing sometimes."

The girl's expression relaxes into a kind smile, her blue eyes glimmering like the topaz stones on the bed of Reedy Creek.

"I'm Ellen," she says, "and this is my sister Elizabeth and brother James."

Joe acknowledges Elizabeth with a tip of his head and shakes James' hand.

"It is for our father we are supposed to be going into town," Ellen begins. "he was unable to make the journey with us, so our neighbour Robert Woods offered to accompany us."

He looks across the road at the young man, sitting hunched in the dirt, the broken piece of iron clutched in his hands. Joe raises his eyebrow.

"Bob is usually much more help to us than this," Elizabeth interjects irritably, noticing his puzzlement.

"I might be able to help," Joe offers, holding Ellen's gaze, causing the girl to blush and avert her eyes.

Smirking at her bashfulness, he turns his attention toward the harness, but the task is quickly obstructed by the pacing of Ah Nam.

"Ah Joe, we go soon," he insists, tugging on Joe's sleeve. Ah Nam's fingernails scrape against the skin of his wrist.

"Haih. We'll go after I look at this. I want to help them back on the road."

"M̀haih," Ah Nam answers with a shake of his head, "we go now!"

Noticing the miner's eyes trained on something across the road, Joe follows his look of derision to the scowling face of Robert Woods.

"He is only angry about the wagon, Ah Nam."

"M̀haih," he responds in disagreement. "he like those fat miners up the road; hate Chinese."

Joe looks up at the clouded heavens and mouths an exasperated prayer, hoping his many hours sitting on the cold pew of St Joseph's might prove for something in the subduing of Ah Nam.

"He needs lesson," the miner declares in response. "and I good teacher."

Suddenly, the anger Joe has attempted to calm all day reaches boiling point and he grasps Ah Nam's shoulders, his fingers driving through his woollen tunic like the talons of an eagle.

"That's enough!" Joe growls angrily. "You will bloody do as I say!" The severity of his words causing the girls to gasp.

Joe crosses the road in an attempt to reason with Robert and his scowl, but before any words are uttered a sharp scream sounds behind him. Spinning around, he notices Ah Nam attempting to grab Ellen's hand, while her and her siblings cower closer to the wagon.

"Why you not go for help? You have legs," Ah Nam demands.

"You leave Ellen alone, you bastard!" Robert shouts from behind him.

Knocking Joe sideways, he sprints across the road. The piece of iron held in his hand like a weapon. Being quick on his feet, Ah Nam avoids the attack and tears a sapling from the ground, swinging it murderously at Robert's head. In an act of defence, Robert slashes Ah Nam with the iron and it cuts across his forehead, leaving a bloody gash. He cries out in pain and pulls off his slipper, swatting Robert's face with it, causing his nose to bleed. The pair wrestle violently in the dirt at Ellen's feet, the girl watching on in horror, her body seemingly paralysed with fear.

Seeing her distress, Joe quickly pulls her away and shields her from the unfolding violence, while Elizabeth snatches James from the roadside and holds him tightly to her chest.

"Ah Nam!" Joe yells, keeping his arms outstretched to protect Ellen. "Ah Nam, that's enough!"

Noticing an opportunity, he grasps the brawling miner by his tunic and wrenches him away. The strength in Joe's arms almost causing him to topple over backwards, as he brings Ah Nam crashing into him.

"Diu lei," he curses, his limbs flailing wildly.

Joe grits his teeth, trying his best to subdue Ah Nam, who continues to thrash under the constraint of his grasp like a calf caught by a rope.

Robert laughs at the scene and begins fidgeting with the piece of iron.

"You're nothing but a dirty yellow fella. Thought you could have your wicked way with Ellen, did you?"

Joe wishes for nothing more than to take the coward on himself, but conceals the hatred behind his clenched jaw.

"Take the girls away," he orders, conscious of the effect the fight is having on Ellen and Elizabeth.

However, Robert ignores the plea and continues provoking Ah Nam, until the miner roars in anger and attempts to free himself from Joe's arms. Wildly, he claws at Joe's face, drawing blood from his cheek.

"Let me kill, let me kill," Ah Nam cries, brutally elbowing Joe in the eye.

Instantly, Joe's grip on Ah Nam loosens and he doubles over in pain, his hand clamped around the right side of his face, which begins to throb. Seizing the opportunity, Ah Nam rushes at Robert with his teeth bared and slipper raised. The pair reassume their ugly fight and receiving another blow to the head with the iron, Ah Nam manages to knock it from Robert's hand and chases him into the scrub.

Joe attempts to reassure the girls, their terrified screams having attracted Israel Abraham and Giles Thrower, who converge on the scene to offer assistance. He begins describing to them the events when there is a sudden rustle of saplings and Ah Nam reappears, stepping out of the scrub like a triumphant boxer, the left side of his face disfigured with blood.

***

Having walked Ellen and her siblings home, Joe and Ah Nam finally arrive into the lantern-lit perimeter of the Chinese Camp.

On seeing Joe and Ah Nam bloodied and bruised, a group of miners eye the pair suspiciously as they walk along the illuminated storefronts. Although Joe is on friendly terms with some of the men, there are many that are not trusting of the Europeans, from whom they are often taunted and harassed. Joe had borne witness to one such incident involving a group of young men who had begun throwing stones at Ah Kee, a miner who shares a hut with Ah Nam. The man had walked down to the creek and commenced washing his feet when the boys descended upon him. They pelted the unsuspecting Ah Kee with stones until a group of his countrymen had come to his aid and rushed at them with shovels.

The smell of cooking rice greets the pair as they arrive outside Ah Nam's hut, the aroma wafting between the gaps in the bark and into Joe's nostrils, causing his empty belly to rumble hungrily.

Ah Nam cups his left hand, imitating a bowl.

"Want eat? Ah Fook good cook."

Joe shakes his head, not wishing to waste any more time, despite the protests from his stomach.

"M̀haih. Ma will have my supper waiting," he lies, knowing he will more than likely be going to bed hungry.

"She will think you been fighting."

Joe allows the comment to pass and taps a finger on his forehead.

"You should go to the hospital for your head in the morning. It'll need bandaging."

"Haih," Ah Nam responds with a bow of his wounded head, "jóutáu, Ah Joe."

"Jóutáu," Joe replies in parting, "good night, Ah Nam."

Waiting until the miner has disappeared inside, Joe glances up at the moon which has risen into the sky and begins to make his way towards the footbridge. Once across it, he looks back in the direction of the Salisbury hut, unable to ignore the tugging at his heart. He knows his mother's wrath will be awaiting him when he walks through the door, so what difference is an hour now?

Joe knocks on the door of the Norfolk native's hut and waits nervously as hushed voices commence within. The door is gingerly opened and Ellen peers into the darkness, yellow light spilling onto Joe's boots.

"Who is it?" she whispers, confusion painted on her face as she tries to recognise the face before her that is shrouded in darkness.

"It's me. Joseph Byrne."

"Joe?"

"I wanted to see you were alright."

Ellen blushes and beckons him in.

"Who be at the door, Nell?"

"Joseph Byrne, sir." Joe announces, stepping forward.

"Young Byrne, is it?" James asks, turning on the bench seat to face Joe. "Cor, blarst me," he continues in surprise, "look at the sight of you."

Joe's cheeks flush self-consciously.

"I got into a bit of a scuffle, sir."

"Oh aye, I can see that, son. Nell and Lizzie told me what happened. That bloody Bob Woods is useless."

"Aye," Joe mumbles. James gestures to his two daughters.

"One of you ought to get off your arse and see to his eye before he makes for home," James begins, "the poor lad will give his mother an awful fright looking like that."

Elizabeth glances upwards from the pot of stew she is tending and rolls her eyes at her father, as Ellen whips around and gathers the necessary items to treat the wounds.

Gesturing for Joe to sit on the end of the wooden bench, Ellen stands over him with a pewter bowl full of water.

"Close your eyes," she whispers; her voice a quiver.

He does as she instructs. The water is cool at his temples as she begins dabbing at his eye and forehead with a dampened cloth. With trembling hand, she squeezes water over the cuts at his cheek and he winces at the sting.

"Did I hurt you?"

Joe shakes his head.

"Don't worry, you didn't."

Walking past the pair to refill his tankard with porter, James pauses and ruffles Ellen's hair.

"You've mobbed a rum'un," he laughs.

Joe's brow furrows at the strange remark.

"Father means I'm making a lot of fuss," Ellen answers, wringing the cloth.

The pair share a smile and Joe wonders whether her heart is beating as frantically as his. For a moment, he longs to allow his fingers to brush against the smoothness of her hand.

As if aware of his thoughts, Ellen blushes, the heat of her breath tickling Joe's cheek.

"All done," she says softly, placing the cloth back into the bowl.

Not wanting to look back on the moment with regret, Joe wraps his fingers gently around hers.

"Thank you, Ellen."

***

Leaving the warmth of the Salisbury hut, Joe trains his eyes down along Byrne Gully, until they come to rest on the shadows of his mother's slab hut, where curls of grey smoke drift into the sky.

As Joe nears the house, a bandicoot scampers from the clump of flowerless iris plants it has been digging amongst and disappears behind the outhouse.

Flickers of yellow light seep between the cracks in the door as Joe stands beneath the veranda, attempting to pluck what courage he has left. He briefly touches the swollen skin around his eye, still tender, despite Ellen's gentle efforts. For a moment, he considers sleeping in the stable, as he has done countless times before when seeking refuge from a tongue lashing, but he knows it would only delay the inevitable. "*Ye have to face yer troubles like a man, Joey,*" his father would say on occasion when Joe would attempt to hide from his mother's reproach.

Guided by his father's voice, he pushes the door open and steps into the warm press of air of the front room, where Margaret sits alone in her rocking chair. He offers her a smile but her expression remains emotionless, as if cast from the granite boulders that surround the valley.

"Just what hour do ye call this, Joseph?" Margaret demands, rising from the rocking chair, her County Clare accent tinged with frustration.

"I'm sorry, ma," Joe offers in apology.

Margaret makes a sweeping gesture with her hand, as if brushing the excuse into the fire.

"Thought it proper to be skulking away without my knowing, did yer?"

Joe hangs his hat against the hook and removes his coat, conscious of the bruising around his eye, which her icy blue eyes meet with a frown. He moves to the table and sits on the wooden bench seat, his gaze trained on the bread crumbs scattered on the table top.

"I didn't mean to be away for so long. I met Nam Shing and he asked for assistance."

"Assistance?" Margaret huffs, pacing behind him. "Yer poor widowed mother gets as little help as a leper, but yer offering charity to half of Beechworth?"

Joe's response swirls in his mind, but the words fail him.

Margaret shakes her head.

"Do yer think me a fool, Joseph? Is that it? Do yer think so little of yer mother that ye can stand there and tell such lies with no effort at all? As if I am nothing more than an orange Bobby."

Joe feels himself falter under her gaze, the pull of the stable like a siren's call, but he holds firm and reaches into his pocket.

"Nam Shing wrote me a note explaining my absence, to give to you."

Noticing the crumpled piece of paper he holds in his hand, Margaret takes it from him and holds it in front of herself. Her blue eyes narrow at the pencilled words, being almost illiterate she struggles to find meaning in the storekeeper's scrawl. Crushing it in her palm she throws Nam Shing's explanation into the fire.

"I know yer trying to make a game of me, Joseph Byrne. Yer sneak away during milking like a common layabout, without even the heart to tell me where yer going. Leaving Patrick to do the work of two, and when yer return, yer be looking like the competitor in a prize fight."

"I'm sorry, ma," Joe says finally, hoping his words sound as sincere as he means them.

"Oh aye," Margaret replies sarcastically, nodding her head. "and I am sure yer are too."

She pauses and flicks her hand at him as if he is little more than a figure of her derision, "Look at the wretched state of yer, how can I ever believe a word that comes out of yer blackened mouth?"

"I was protecting Ellen," Joe answers sharply, the emotion catching in his throat. "I wanted to see that she made it home safe and I felt it right that I stay and explain her absence to her father."

"Who's Ellen?"

"James Salisbury's daughter. They live opposite the creek. I had to double back with Ah Nam before I could return home."

For a fleeting moment the hardness in Margaret's eyes waver.

"Yer protected her?"

Joe nods.

"Their neighbour Robert Woods, and Ah Nam from the camp, started fighting, and there was nothing I could do."

Margaret takes up position across from her son at the table and looks down at her knotted hands.

"Look ma, I'm not Denny," Joe says quietly, his voice pleading for understanding, "I am 16 years old. I'm not a little kid anymore."

She lifts her head and settles her eyes on the auburn wisps of his moustache, but says nothing. Joe is unsure what to make of her response, but knows she is too proud to take back the things she has said.

Margaret rises from her chair and gestures a hand towards the stew pot that hangs over the hearth.

"I'll dish some stew from the pot. Yer belly must be hollow."

Spooning chunks of potato and meat onto a plate, Margaret hands it to Joe. The creases in the corners of her mouth giving away the slight smile that rests on her lips.

***

Having had his fill of mutton, Joe strips down to his night clothes and tiptoes towards his bed, careful not to wake Paddy and Denny who slumber soundly. He slides beneath the woollen blanket and stares up at the calico, watching the makeshift ceiling breathing in the gloom with each gust of wind that whistles through the slabs. His exhausted mind drifts to Ellen Salisbury, her tender smile helping him fall peacefully into sleep.

Acknowledgments

Ah Nam has been a labour of love, blood, sweat and tears since the narrative first drew breath in December 2019. What began as a scribbled note on the timeline of Joe Byrne's life, has transformed into a story which has given back life to those whose names and stories have become lost to the deep fog of time.

I have learnt so much about these people and their lives, and I will always be eternally grateful for the lessons I have learnt while gathering their stories. For these people, Beechworth and the surrounding country was their home, and I hope that with the aid of this narrative, their lives within Beechworth and the Woolshed Valley may be brought to the fore. I also hope that after reading this narrative you are enticed to picture them within your mind's eye. Perhaps while taking the Woolshed Valley Touring Route self-guided drive, you may pass a young Joe Byrne walking with Ah Nam, just before the pair are stopped by the wagon that is parked along the roadside...

Now to the acknowledgments, it is Ah Nam I wish to firstly recognise, for it is his actions and character which has influenced this narrative and without him this story would not be.

I also wish to acknowledge the two main influences on the narrative, Joe Byrne and Aaron Sherritt. Their lives have inspired me to such a great extent that I could not imagine a life void of their stories. In particular, it is Joe I wish to acknowledge, as it is his life that has given me an abundance of influence and strength when I have needed it the most.

Finally, 'Ah Nam' is currently held within your hands because of the encouragement and love of my partner, Aidan Phelan. He is the biggest supporter of my Joe Byrne related research and writing, and keeps the whiskey in my glass when I need it. Without his advice, guidance and encouragement, the writing of this narrative would have been a daunting and lonely task.

Aidan is also the illustrator of my work and I am eternally grateful to have his beautiful pictures beside my writing. I thank him for again shaping my words into powerful and emotive illustrations.

Georgina Stones, 2021.

An Outlaw's Journal

Behind the Journal

The narrative has been written and researched with the aim of shining a light on an incident in Joe's life, which up until now, has been lost to history. With the aid of Trove, a resource which is invaluable for researchers such as myself, I located an assault case from the 7th of April 1873, between a young man named Robert Woods and a Chinese miner called Ah Nam.

At the time, I was not looking for specifics in the *Ovens and Murray Advertiser* that related to Joe, rather I was reading through the issue out of my own curiosity. This all changed, however, when my blue eyes settled on the name, 'Joseph Burns'. Initially, I did not think much of it, as Joe was a 'Byrne', not a 'Burns', but my position changed when I flicked back to the reporting of the Ah Suey murder case from 1872 and saw that at the inquest Joe's surname was written as 'Burnes'. Furthermore, Joe was not the only one to have his surname misspelt at the assault trial, as the Salisbury siblings, became 'Salsbury', highlighting that because the majority of the spelling of names was done phonetically, there was always discrepancies in the way they were spelt.

While the incident has remained unknown until now, it makes it no less significant in Joe's life. The meeting of Ah Nam along the Woolshed Road, the miner's fight with Robert Woods and the consequent trial, provides a great insight into Joe's relationship with the Chinese of Sebastopol and his relationship with Ellen Salisbury. It is a pivotal moment in the 16-year old's life, where we are given our first possible recorded meeting between Joe and Ellen, a young woman who would go on to become his sweetheart and one of his biggest supporter's during his outlawry. As the meeting between Joe and Ellen is so important, I wanted to convey it as such within the narrative and show how it sparked a deeper connection in the months and years following.

The story also demonstrates Joe's ability to stand on the side of his Chinese mate, despite the anti-Chinese sentiment present at the trial and reporting of the case in the *Ovens and Murray Advertiser*. A day after the fight, when Ah Nam presented himself at the hospital with head wounds, the paper referred to Ah Nam as 'Broken China' and made the following report:

> *'Ah Nam — not the Chinese interpreter — but a resident of the Woolshed was brought to the Ovens District Hospital on Saturday, suffering from severe wounds to the head inflicted, it is alleged, by an iron bar, wielded by a European named Woods. Two girls, on whom Ah Nam had, or fancied he had, some claim, it is reported, had been journeying with Woods on a wagon, when the ardent Celestial endeavoured to stop their progress [...] and the result of this attempt was a row in which Ah Nam came off second best.'*

Furthermore, despite Elizabeth Salisbury and Robert Woods attempting to incriminate Ah Nam in their evidence, claiming he had said he would kill Robert, Joe stood by his Chinese mate and denied such a threat had been made, even in the face of so much anti-Chinese sentiment within the courtroom. This mateship and loyalty are two themes I felt integral to highlight within the narrative, as it helps explain why many Chinese continued to help and support him as an outlaw.

Within the narrative, I believed it imperative that I highlighted the forgotten people of Beechworth, rather than simply generate imaginary names. To do this, I extensively read the reporting of trials, advertisements and reminisces from Beechworth locals. This allowed me to include individuals such as Joe's teenage mate James Tatham, women such as Sarah Payne and Ettie Noble and storekeeper Daniel McNamara. Consulting the *Ovens and Murray Advertiser* also allowed preciseness in my recording of the weather Joe would have walked in on that Friday morning in April and letters to the editor gave me general context as to the state of the Woolshed Road and the lack of signposts leading from Sebastopol to the township of Beechworth.

The fractured relationship between Joe and his mother Margaret, was another issue I wished to explore and highlight, and it is a theme which weaves through the entirety of the narrative.

Finally, as Joe spoke and understood Cantonese, I felt it integral to include phrases and words in this language, which I have endeavoured to highlight within the narrative as much as I can. This was included, also, as a way of capturing realism and to show respect to the spoken language of the Chinese miners, cooks and storekeepers who had emigrated from Hong Kong. The internet site, *Omniglot*, has proven imperative in this understanding and can be sourced at: *https://omniglot.com/language/phrases/cantonese.php*.

The Importance of Ellen Salisbury

While it is not known when the paths of Ellen Salisbury and Joe Byrne first crossed, their first documented meeting was in 1873, as depicted within the narrative of *Ah Nam*. After the incident along the Woolshed Road, Joe and Ellen were noted sweethearts, with Ellen employed as a domestic servant at Mrs. Batchelor's Hotel at Sebastopol. She was also friendly with Joe's sister, Kate Byrne, and regularly spent time at the Byrne house, despite her fear of Margaret. (*Royal Commission*, q.14190, p.517.) Ellen was also at the Byrne home when Aaron Sherritt gifted a bay filly to Kate, his sweetheart. (*Ovens and Murray Advertiser*, July 29, 1879.)

In Max Brown's book *Australian Son*, he shares an interview he had with an old Beechworth resident who had been a girlfriend of Joe's during their teenage years. While no name was given as to the identity of the woman, using context clues, it is plausible to surmise that the woman may have been Ellen Byron (née Salisbury).

With memory of Joe still clear within her mind, she recounted the following to Brown:

There was no harm in Joe. He was a nice boy. He brought me two curlews, but the mother bird followed them down. When night came, they commenced to squeal so we let them go. Then he brought me a lamb. You never knew where he got it; and it followed me around for years, even after he himself was dead. He was a nice, quiet boy, not flash, and a fine horseman. He would come in at any old hour to stay for the night, and my father would say, "Whose horse have you got tonight?" And Joe would tell him.

MAX BROWN, AUSTRALIAN SON, 2005, P. 59

After Ellen's marriage to Martin Byron in July 1876, officiated while Joe was serving a 6-month sentence with Aaron for cattle stealing, her loyalty and support for her teenage sweetheart never once wavered. From late October 1878 to June 1880, while Joe's life was outlawed, Ellen regularly supplied him with provisions and was one of his most loyal sympathisers, despite the consequences that came with supporting him.

During the Royal Commission, Ann Sherritt asserted:

I had heard that [the Kelly gang] were supplied with provisions from a woman that lived near Chiltern that was an old sweetheart of Byrne's.

ROYAL COMMISSION, Q.13210, P. 477

While an outlaw, Joe frequently called at the Black Dog Creek, near Chiltern, where Ellen's husband, Martin Byron, ran the aptly named shanty of 'Lord Byron's'. Here, Joe would be given food, shelter and relayed information regarding the movements of his foes. One such visit was made in the days before Joe and Dan Kelly had left for the New South Wales township of Jerilderie.

News of this visit had soon reached the ears of Superintendent Hare, with him commenting:

> ***"I found that Joe Byrne and Dan Kelly had been seen by others going in the direction of the Murray a couple of days before, and that they had called for supplies at a shanty where Byrne was well known."***

FRANCIS AUGUSTUS HARE, THE LAST OF THE BUSHRANGERS, 1895, P.141

While the exact name of the shanty was omitted by Hare, there can be little doubt the shanty he referred to was 'Lord Byron's', where Joe was very much "well known."

Another recorded visit to Ellen and her husband's shanty was in May 1880, when it was reported to Detective Ward by a police spy. As with before, Joe was again joined by Dan, but on this occasion, however, it was described that the two outlaws were "miserable and ragged" and greatly "in want of food". Just as Ellen would have done in previous visits, the young woman ushered the gaunt and hungry pair inside and allowed them to warm themselves by the fire while she prepared them both a meal. Soon after this was eaten, Joe gave Ellen a letter he had written for his mother, Margaret, which she promised to deliver, and on the outlaws' departure, gave her old sweetheart "a lot of food" and other provisions to tide them over. (*Royal Commission*, q.13858, p.503.)

In September 1879, James Wallace, Joe's old schoolmate, supplied information to Detective Ward in reference to a person who lived in Chiltern and who "knows where Joe Byrne can be seen." This "person" would have undoubtedly been Ellen or Martin Byron.

Ellen Salisbury may be a sympathiser whose significance has been largely forgotten about, but this in itself is why her inclusion within the story of *Ah Nam* was imperative for me. Of course, the telling of the incident cannot be undertaken without her, as she was, after all, one of only four people to give evidence. However Ellen's importance within Joe's life extended far more than simply this event. She remained loyal to Joe all throughout his young life. From a teenager 'borrowing' horses with Aaron Sherritt, to his life as a hunted outlaw, she was one of the only constants within his life. Her role as a sympathiser is something that should never be undermined, for she was willing to risk it all for Joe, as indeed she did.

The Trial

It is important to note how Joe Byrne's evidence is so different to Elizabeth Salisbury's in the subsequent trial of Ah Nam and Robert Woods, as he doesn't portray Ah Nam as being violent. It really highlights the attitudes towards the Chinese at that time that Elizabeth would say that Ah Nam had threatened to kill Robert, while Joe, who was sympathetic to the Chinese, did not mention such a threat at all.

In the narrative that I constructed, based on the available evidence, I was careful to avoid simply taking Joe's word for it, as I wanted a rounded portrayal of Ah Nam and the situation that landed everyone in court. I was sure to keep in mind the anti-Chinese sentiment, but also kept in mind that Joe, being a mate of Ah Nam, wouldn't want to paint him as the villain. It is hard to know if Ah Nam was more at fault than Robert Woods just from the witness accounts, as there is obviously conflicting information, so I had to make a judgement call and find the balance between the perspectives to find the most credible interpretation.

In the reporting of Ah Nam's own version of events, we see that it was Robert Woods that struck the first blow, and the fact that people were ready and willing to believe that Ah Nam would have approached the girls with bad intentions goes further to demonstrating the fear and hatred of the Chinese that was present.

I find it interesting how constrained the reporting is compared to the heightened tension of the actual moment that it is describing. It was obviously a very brutal thing. Ah Nam was bandaged from the wounds gained in the assault, and it wasn't reported until he had been hospitalised as a result of the attack, despite other such brawls being reported even without the combatants having to seek medical attention. Yet you don't get any sense of the savagery from the writing. It is also noteworthy because the papers were always eager to publish reports on brawls between the Chinese, rather more so than other ethnic groups, and for the initial report on Ah Nam's case, that of a Chinese man being brutally assaulted by a white, to be given the headline "Broken China" as some attempt at humour, really underscores the way that the media reflected the views of the white society. The very emotionless tone of the report, as shown below, really got me thinking about how Joe would have responded to what he was seeing during the incident. It was important for me as a writer, as much as a historian, to go beyond merely the words, to find the emotional truth behind what was being portrayed.

The trial of the assault as reported within the *Ovens and Murray Advertiser* is as follows:

Robert Woods, a rather inoffensive-looking man, was charged with having assaulted Ah Nam, who appeared in court with his head bandaged up.

Elizabeth Salisbury, a girl of fifteen- or sixteen-years of age, residing at Sebastopol, said that on Friday evening she was with defendant, when he was driving his wagon on the Woolshed-road. her brother and sister were with her, after having gone about a mile and a half, defendant missed a piece of iron from the saddle: they all went back to look for it, a and found it lying on the road; after they had found the piece of iron, they all sat down on the road-side; when sitting there a Chinaman came out of the bushes, and said something to Bob in Chinese, and then struck him with his fist and afterwards with a slipper. Bob struck him with the piece of iron produced, and then ran away: the Chinaman broke a stick and ran after him. In answer to defendant, witness said that she heard the Chinaman say he would kill him. Ellen Salisbury, a younger sister, corroborated the evidence of the previous witness.

Joseph Burns, a labourer, said that on Friday evening he met the complainant, Ah Nam, and with him proceeded towards the Woolshed; on their way they overtook defendant and the previous witnesses; some words passed between them, when the Chinaman took off his slipper and struck defendant about the head; he struck him several times, and defendant hit him back with the piece of iron he had in his hand; the Chinaman procured a sapling, and defendant ran away. In answer to defendant, witness said that he did not hear the Chinaman say he would kill him; defendant said to him to take the Chinaman away, as he did not want to strike him.

Dr Mousse gave evidence as to the nature of the wounds received by defendant, neither of them was of a dangerous character, and from the instrument used it was probable that one blow had caused them both.

Ah Nam, who appeared like the man who had won the fight, said that he went after the girls to ask them to come and look after the place, when defendant interfered and struck him with a piece of iron; he had not struck the defendant first. The bench said there was no doubt the defendant had received considerable provocation, but not sufficient to justify him in using such a weapon as that produced.

Verdict - Fined 40s, with the alternative of fourteen days' imprisonment.

Aaron Sherritt, James Wallace and Jimmy Tatham

Aaron Sherritt, James Wallace and James Tatham were prominent figures within Joe Byrne's life, and as such feature prominently within *Ah Nam*. In fact, no retelling of Joe's life can be undertaken without the inclusion of Aaron in particular, the larrikin from Sheepstation Creek, as his life from boyhood into adulthood, and even death, was heavily intertwined with that of Joe.

While little about the early life of these young men is recorded, this snippet from the *Singleton Argus* from 1924 provides some context into the importance of Aaron and James Wallace in Joe's story:

> ***"A name that looms large in the criminal records of Australia is that of Aaron Sherritt. Physically, he was a man in a thousand, and his beautifully proportioned limbs were the envy of his companions. As a lad he attended the State School at Woolshed, and had two bosom companions Joe Byrne and another lad, James Wallace. On leaving school these three youths remained, almost to the last, the same trusting friends as in their happy boyhood days. Each was possessed of a fairly good education; in fact, James became a State School teacher and served in the Victorian Education Department."***
>
> SINGLETON ARGUS, 12 APRIL 1924, P.5

The dynamic of the boys was something I very much wanted to explore within the narrative of *Ah Nam* in order to contextualise Joe's behaviour. Of the three, Aaron was very much the leader, while Joe was more than happy to simply follow Aaron's lead, and James Wallace was more keen to keep his nose clean. This tendency to follow that

Joe exhibited around Aaron, and later Ned Kelly, would prove to be his undoing quite often, and in the context of *Ah Nam* it was important to show how easily his path could be diverted by others, even when he had the best intentions. Though he intends to simply pop into town for a bit of reading then sneak home to do his chores, Aaron derails that plan with his impulsive trip to the Burke, then, just when Joe seems to be regaining control, Nam Shing diverts his path again, only this time the reason is one that Joe should feel less ashamed of telling his mother about.

It was Aaron Sherritt's assertiveness and bravado that led Joe by the nose into all sorts of trouble. He was naturally charismatic, and as Joe was a fiercely loyal and devoted friend, such that he rarely, if ever, questioned Aaron's ideas. Although Aaron often led Joe astray, his loyalty to Joe was equal to Joe's for him, and would remain so for the rest of his life.

Yet, Aaron seemingly lacked the ability to comprehend how his actions could affect others, as at around this time in his life he was heavily involved in duffing with John Phelan, the local poundmaster, and had been attempting to gain a butcher's licence under a false identity, incriminating one of his Chinese associates in the process. Aaron was as carefree as one could imagine, and as none of his misdeeds had caught up with him yet it seemed to embolden him further. Aaron and Joe had known each other for many years by the point at which the *Ah Nam* incident took place, and as Aaron had recently acquired a selection of his own Joe was spending large amounts of his time there. For this reason, it is easy to imagine Mrs. Byrne feeling as if Joe was deliberately neglecting his duties on the family farm, yet Joe was simply helping his best mate to take care of his selection.

On his visits into Beechworth, Aaron's clothing choice was often a point of interest for many within the Beechworth community, with Richard Warren, son of the proprietor of the *Ovens and Murray Advertiser* of the same name, recalling his appearance in the *Australian Monthly*, June 1949:

"Flash as Lucifer, dressed up to kill [...] anyone seeing him coming down Ford Street would ask, 'Who the hell's this? Some advance agent for the circus?'"

Meanwhile Joe Byrne and James Wallace were rather more soberly dressed in their town clothes and low-crowned hats.

The story of Aaron Sherritt and Joe Byrne extends far further than what the scope of this narrative allows and it does not warrant a full recounting here. Suffice it to say that this is only a sampling of their tale.

James Wallace, by comparison, could best be described as a "fair-weather friend". Wallace was, perhaps, as self-centred as Aaron, but whereas Aaron's self-absorption came from a place of carelessness, Wallace's was more about self-aggrandisement. He was petty and willing to do whatever was necessary to advance his own situation, as evidenced by his behaviour during the Kelly Outbreak. His two-facedness at that time would be in an effort to gain either reward money or other payouts from the police at the expense of his boyhood chums. He was as likely to inform on the Sherritts as sympathisers as he was to dob in the Byrnes whenever he discovered that they had been visited by Joe. Though we don't see this on display as brazenly in the early days, I hint at it in his mannerisms in the narrative of *Ah Nam*.

In September of 1873, only a few months after the events of *Ah Nam*, Wallace would gain a plum job as the schoolmaster at the Hurdle Creek School. At the time this story is set, Wallace was employed as a teacher's assistant under Thomas Trembath at the El Dorado Common School. No doubt, at this time he would have been trying to distance himself from Joe and Aaron more, given their behaviour could have tarnished his blossoming reputation. In 1874 he would get married, by which time he had more or less broken ties with Aaron and Joe. It would be Joe's outlawry four years later that would bring James Wallace back to the Woolshed looking for a slice of the reward money.

During the period in which *Ah Nam* is set, the trio of Joe, Aaron and James, was familiar around the streets of Beechworth, and they were often joined by another youth named James "Jimmy" Tatham. While details of the friendship of Joe and James Tatham are scarce, it is probable the pair first met while at mass at St Joseph's Catholic Church, Beechworth. When interviewed by the *Healesville and Yarra Glen Guardian* as an old man, Tatham stated, "The Byrnes were a very decent family. I saw Byrne's sister (Kate) confirmed in the Beechworth Catholic Church."

Tatham also worked for Beechworth grocer William Greer, as mentioned elsewhere in the same article, giving a much clearer idea of the context of his friendship with Byrne and company:

> ***"After the grocery shop was closed for the day, [he] mixed about with the boys of the town. His pals were Joe Byrne and Aaron Sherritt, both well-known names in the history of the Kelly uprising. As a matter of fact, Sherritt worked for Jimmy's father, helping him with the bricks."***
>
> HEALESVILLE AND YARRA GLEN GUARDIAN, 16 JUNE 1934, P.3.

Tatham had many memories of life during the Kelly Outbreak many years later, including of the Chinese and the prostitutes that co-habited with them, but this is all that has been preserved of his youth with the boys from the Woolshed.

As we can see, these three young men in Joe's life have wildly contrasting personalities, but it was important to include them in the story. Not only is it a chance to help preserve them, but they are also reflections of Joe's journey in the narrative: Aaron is his whimsy and desire to be carefree, James Wallace is his fear of being judged and desire to slink away, Tatham is his industriousness and dedication to completing the task set for him. In a sense, this is Joe's whole personality in a nutshell. It highlights the way in which those who we connect with are often a reflection of ourselves.

Ettie Noble, Sarah Payne, and the Women of Spring Creek

While the real Ah Nam was noted to be living with a woman named Ellen Doyle, it was another young woman I wished to feature within the narrative of *Ah Nam*; Esther Noble. Ettie, as she was commonly known, was a prostitute who resided with Sarah Payne, the notorious brothel madam of the Spring Creek Chinese Camp, but also flitted between the huts of Ah Hen, Ah Ling, Ah Sin and Ah Tow. Ettie was a common figure within the Beechworth Courthouse, with fines for obscene language, fighting with other prostitutes, and drunkenness becoming routine within the young woman's life. Like many other women within the camp, Ettie was an alcoholic, using drink to cope with the hardship and violence that enveloped her life. Being intoxicated was described by Ettie as a 'pleasant sensation', which acted as a shield against the trauma.

It was from discovering and learning about Ettie's life which prompted me to include her in the narrative. Although Ah Nam would definitively be romantically linked to Ellen Doyle after the events dramatised in this book, I felt that this was a perfect opportunity to depict the relationships between the maligned Chinese and prostitutes of Beechworth, with Ettie as the figurehead that represented the affinity these two marginalised groups had for each other that so often led to romance and companionship. The historical Ettie may never have met the real Ah Nam, but what we do know is that she was most comfortable with the Chinese, who respected her and treated her like a woman, whereas the European men treated her poorly; in fact when her future partner, Louis Solomon, a white man, took to violently abusing Ettie, Ah Tow tried to intervene to protect her. Sadly, this would not be enough to save her and Louis would go on to kill Ettie on 10 October 1899, when she was aged only thirty six, after striking a blow to her head that caused a fatal hemorrhage.

When I began reading the articles that documented her misadventures, I could hardly believe what I was reading. How could such a fascinating and notable person in the history of Beechworth go forgotten for so long? It became imperative to me that I created an avenue through which I could revive her memory and preserve her story, and she is now forever remembered within the story of *Ah Nam*.

In appearance, Ettie was marred by several scars on her face and chest, highlighting the violence experienced within her life. She also evidently suffered from a range of health problems brought on by her heavy drinking. At her inquest, she was described by the coroner, Abraham Haynes, thus:

> ***The body was that of a female, aged about 36 years. The body was well nourished, and there were several old scars on the face and chest. On the left side of the face there was a recent bruise which extended to the left temple. On opening the head I found a recent hemorrhage between the membranes of the brain. The hemorrhage was behind the bruise on the temple. The right kidney was congested, the left kidney was fairly healthy. The heart was somewhat fatty, and showed signs of chronic congestion.***
>
> OVENS AND MURRAY ADVERTISER, 21 OCTOBER 1899, P. 4

This description really talks about the life she lived. If she were any "respectable" woman around Beechworth she could hardly have been expected to be carrying around these scars. Her hard drinking and her almost constant brawling with other prostitutes and men defined her life, but also demonstrate that she was a survivor in a harsh world that would just as soon chew her up and spit her out.

In many ways this brings to my mind one of my own ancestors, Ann Tully, who was forced to prostitute herself in order to survive, and needed to constantly be drunk to forget her life as a convict, spent in the Tasmanian female factories, and the abusive relationship she had with her husband George. If Ann had have lived around Beechworth she would have been one of those women on Spring Creek, so this was a deeply personal connection, for me, to the lives that these women lived.

These women were filed down by harsh treatment; the way that they lived and acted was out of survival. They did not have the luxury of wealth or social standing to rely on to preserve themselves, and fell on whatever calling they could to keep themselves fed, clothed and housed. It didn't matter to them that the money came from what others considered deplorable, of ill-repute or low morals. Their trade was considered a "social evil", something that couldn't just be hidden away. The respectable people of Beechworth frequently complained about these *unseemly* prostitutes coming out onto Camp Street among the masses, or even running naked through the streets on occasion, highlighting the pervasiveness of the issue. It was discussed as being the byproduct of a society that would rather try to conceal its dirty laundry, than work to address the systemic problems that resulted in young ladies becoming "fallen women".

This brings us to Little Bourke Street celebrity, Sarah Payne, who took many young women under her wing, including Ettie Noble, and employed them in the carnal arts in her Spring Creek brothel. Payne was frequently in the courts for fighting with her prostitutes and Chinese men, and some of her biggest rivals were European women who had married Chinese miners, such as Lizzie Ah Fee (née White), otherwise known to Beechworth locals as "The Tiger", who she notably came into conflict with on several occasions.

An incident that illustrates the often bizarre incidents in Payne's life that were frequently brought before the courts can be seen in her January 1875 case against a local Chinese man named Ah Chung, who she had charged with "wilfully and feloniously setting fire to a dwelling house", following that man's consumption of a quantity of opium in her brothel. Sarah Payne described the incident in her deposition:

> ***On the 3rd inst. Ah Chung was at my place, before dark. He stayed about a quarter of an hour. He then went away and returned a second time, when he stayed about an hour and a half smoking opium. He did not want to remain. I had no words with him. He had often been in the house before. I had known him for some time on Spring Creek. The next morning he came to my house again, and was in the skillion at the back. I did not go into the room whilst he was there. I heard no noise, but distinctly heard a match struck, and a young woman who lived with me told me that the house was on fire. I went to the fire, and threw a cup of tea on it and extinguished it.***
>
> OVENS AND MURRAY ADVERTISER, 7 JANUARY 1875, P. 3

This case was thrown out of court for lack of evidence and labelled "absurd". Sarah was often caught up in cases that would seem too frivolous or ridiculous to bring before a court these days, more often than not due to things such as her prostitutes being overheard using obscene language.

In August 1877, multiple charges of assault and damaging property were placed against Sarah Payne, Lizzie Rowley, Annie Mason, Ah Fee and Elizabeth "The Tiger" White after a massive brawl at Spring Creek. The Tiger set upon Payne and company, with her husband joining in and allegedly beating Sarah Payne with a heavy opium pipe while The Tiger pulled Payne's hair out. The Tiger also threw a flower pot at Rowley. After many witnesses made their, often conflicting, statements the case was adjourned with all defendants made to keep the peace "towards all her majesty's subjects" for twelve months or forfeit £20, with a £10 surety.

Her self-righteous conduct made her stand out amongst the many respectable, and not-so-respectable, people of Beechworth society. She always had things to say about the other women who were often her staff, or indeed rivals in the trade, and her sharp-tongued tendencies would see her charged or sentenced on a myriad of things on a frequent basis, to the extent that the newspapers referred to her as "notorious". In terms of her influence in Spring Creek, she easily held as much sway as the more widely respected entrepreneurs such as William Nam Shing, albeit for less socially acceptable reasons. She was known by just about everybody in the community there, and she cared not if it was fame for good reasons or bad reasons. So long as she could continue to make money by plying the trade of her girls, that was all she cared about in the end.

These wanton women played a very important part in the foundation of Beechworth's history. It is likely that Joe Byrne would have been very familiar with them and their activities, and likely would have made connections with their ilk in the Woolshed as well. Like Joe, they were interwoven with the Chinese community and other aspects of life in Beechworth, with their infamy ensuring that their names have been preserved, even if it is for the wrong reasons. Their independence and refusal to simply play by society's rulebook ensured that their lives were always interesting, but unfortunately also played a big part in the tragedy of their lives. By examining these characters we can learn about what kinds of people populated Beechworth and surrounds during this tumultuous period and how their personalities are reflected in the culture, environment and people that remain in Beechworth now.

Wanted, Sign-Posts: A Letter to the Editor

Source: Ovens and Murray Advertiser (Beechworth, Vic. : 1855 - 1918), Tuesday 18 March 1873, page 3

ORIGINAL CORRESPONDENCE.

———

WANTED, SIGN-POSTS.

To the Editor of The Ovens and Murray Advertiser.

Sir, — Knowing well how ready you are at all times to sympathise with the unfortunate, I have no hesitation in giving my bitter grievance before you. I am a stranger in these parts, and alas that I should say it — but the truth must he told— my geographical education has been sadly neglected. I never saw the Geodetic map in the Chiltern paper in my life until to-day, when sad experience jeered at my ignorance. Having heard of Beechworth; what a pretty place it was; so charmingly situated; so healthy; the people so charitable; ladies so pretty, and, what's better than all, articles of wearing apparel — I mean trowsers and shirts, socks, &c. — so very cheap, I resolved at all hazards to pay a visit to this modern Athens. Accordingly, I saved up all my tin, never drunk a drop, except once, when under heavy pressure; even then I was cunning enough to put some water in my gingerbeer for fear it would go to my head; so, steady and sober, with thirty shillings in pocket, I started off for Beechworth. My journey for about twelve miles passed off pretty well, nice scenery and such like, and — I was nearly forgetting — such a lot ond [*sic*] variety of roads. Well, I went on till

I came up to a hut, seeing a man at the door, I smiled and said, "Good morning! how far to Beechworth ? " "Is it to Beechworth you're goin' honey? " "Yes, sir," says I. "Sure, if you walk till doomsday you'll never get there, it's to Chiltern you're goin' sure." The man's serious and respectable appearance precluded the thought of practical joking. "If yon go hack on the road for about two miles and a-half, and take the road to the left, you'll be right." I thanked the man for his courtesy, and turned my back on him. I jogged on, very much out of temper, — for you must know that the road is all up hill and stony. I saw ever so many roads going to the left, but I resolved not to be tempted, but, to follow my friend's direction. Virtue was soon rewarded, for, after about an hour's walking, sure enough there was a road turning slap to the left. I could not help giving an involuntary "hurrah for Beechworth," so on I tripped gaily. What was my surprise when, after about twenty minutes' walk, I came upon a spot that I had seen before, about half an hour previously. I knew it at a glance; for there, in large red block letters, stared me in the face, "Go and buy of Finch, Ford-street, Beechworth." I naturally, with the curiosity of my race, looked at this red phenomenon. "Well, well," said I, " I have seen all this before, only it was in black, and this is in red, — a trifle in itself; but I must be off, for it is getting late. Let's see, — I am to take the first road to the left: of course." So after turning round a few times, I took the best-looking road to the left. "Here is off for Beechworth!" I must confess not in the best of humors, for I was hungry and tired: however, I whistled a favorite tune of mine, and put on a spurt. No: it cannot be, — what do mine eyes behold ? "The Woolshed Inn," and " Go and buy of Finch," &c. Horror of horrors! I passed that way this very morning. So I went to the Inn, and drowned my sorrow. In about half-an-hour I started again, fortified by "a liquor," and good directions. I was tired and footsore by this time, but I had plenty of pluck, so I kept on, determined to see Beechworth or perish. By and Bye that rascally red "Go and buy" glared upon me. "Aha, old friend, you don't confuse, me again this time if I know it, I shall keep straight on my road as I was told at the Woolshed Inn; but still there seemed to be so many roads straight on, I wonder which of them it is, perhaps that official-looking document over against that tree will tell, *faugh*, "D. Wright has cheap drapery; &c., &c." Now, sir, what do those rascals mean by mocking people in that fashion? Sticking on every tree to go and buy at their places in Ford-street, Beechworth; but, confound them, why don't they tell where Beechworth is." I am surprised, sir, that your enlightened Shire Council (who have shown their wisdom in not following, the vulgar custom of older shires who disfigure the picturesqueness of intersecting roads with, wooden posts having gaunt arms sticking out with impertinent suggestions which way a person should go, as if a Christian did'nt [*sic*] know better than a wooden post.) I say, sir, that a body of men who have shown such praiseworthy forbearance ought not to tolerate such an outrage upon society as these unfeeling individuals — Finch and Wright, I mean — are guilty of. — I am, sir, yours angrily;

VERITAS.'

[Our correspondent in somewhat quaint fashion has touched on a veritable grievance; the roads to the neighborhood of Beechworth are puzzling even to a resident, and must be much more so to a stranger. A few fingerposts here and there would save much unnecessary travel, and the expenditure of many hard words. — Ed. O. & M. A.]

Mr. James Tatham's Reminiscences

Source: Healesville and Yarra Glen Guardian (Vic. : 1900 - 1942) 16 June 1934, page 3.

Another Healesville Link with the Kellys

—

MR. JAMES TATHAM'S REMINISCENCES

Probably no other article that has appeared in "The Guardian" of recent years has aroused so much interest as that dealing with Mr. Edward Barrett's recollections of the notorious Kelly Gang, which was published about a month ago. A great number of our readers have commented on the article, some saying that the details given were correct, others that it was akin to a fabrication. But all have agreed that it was interesting, and of the class of reading matter not often found in a country newspaper. As stated at the time, we hope to publish further similar articles. Shortly after Mr. Barrett's story appeared we were stopped in Symonds by our old friend, Mr. James Tatham. "Been reading that Kelly Gang yarn of yours in the paper," he said. "Mighty interesting reading, but many of the statements were wrong. Perhaps your informant's memory failed him. You know, it was a mighty long time ago that the Kellys roamed the ranges, and a man's memory is likely to trick him after all those years." We compromised with Mr. Tatham by asking him to give his version of the story. At first he was reluctant to do so, on the grounds that he did not like to be brought into the limelight. But when he told us that he had actually worn the famous suit of armour used by Ned Kelly, we used our best powers of persuasion to induce Mr. Tatham to tell his tale as a matter of historical record. We made an appointment with him to come down to the office, sit himself comfortably in the easy chair we keep in reserve for very special callers, and tell readers what he remembered of the doughty days "when the Kellys rode."

WHAT HAPPENED IN THE BAR PARLOUR.

Mr. Tatham kept his promise, and herewith follows the result of the interview. Mr. Tatham first saw the light of day at Chiltern (Vic.), 76 years ago. Subsequently the family moved to Beechworth, where, as a lad, Mr. Tatham joined the grocery business of Mr. Greer, as assistant. The shop was directly opposite the famous Beechworth gaol, many of the bricks used in the building of which were made by young Jimmy Tatham's father. Well, time, as it has a way of doing, went on, and the next picture shows us Jimmy now grown into a young man of 24-quite a dandy of the the period — and still in the employ of Mr. Greer. Beechworth is described by Mr. Tatham as being "a roaring town" in those days. Gold was the magnet that drew hundreds to seek their fortune there. The town was over-run with the riff-raff of a nation. There was a Chinese quarter, populated with a dense horde of Celestials living in real Chinese style. Of course Jimmy, after the grocery shop was closed for the day, mixed about with the boys of the town. His pals were Joe Byrne and Aaron Sherritt, both well known names in the history of the Kelly uprising. As a matter of fact, Sherritt worked for Jimmy's father, helping him with the bricks. One evening — a Saturday — Jimmy and his pals were playing billiards in Allan's Star Hotel, in Ford street. This was prior to the apprehension of the Kellys, who were then on the warpath. Mr. Allan came into the billiard room and showed the young men a handful of fourpenny pieces, which he said the Kellys had no doubt taken from the banks. This, of course, was intriguing news.

THE MAN ON THE CORNER.

Another day, when Jimmy was at work in the grocery, Mr. Greer called him to the door and pointed to a strange man lounging at the corner of the street. "That man looks mighty like Ned Kelly to me," Jimmy's boss whispered to him. This made Jimmy's hair stand on end. "We'd better not, leave any cash around to-night," the boss continued. "Make sure you lock the store up properly, Jimmy." The strange part of this story is that some time later, when the police rounded up Ned Kelly and brought him to Beechworth to stand his trial, both Jimmy and his boss saw that their suppositions about the strange man on the corner had been correct. The man in the box in the Beechworth court was the same man they had seen hanging about the street. This made Jimmy's hair stand on end again.

NED KELLY LAUGHS AT HIS TRIAL.

During the Kelly trial at Beechworth Jimmy Tatham and his boss used to take it in turns to be in the court, where they watched the grim proceedings from beginning to end. Mr. Tatham says that Ned Kelly took things very lightly during the ordeal, and showed a carefree and laughing face to the world. The streets outside were packed with dense crowds and Ned had plenty of sympathisers. There were many undesirable white women living with the Chinese. When Ned Kelly was led by the police to and from the courthouse, these women would heckle the police unmercifully and call out all kinds of endearments to Ned.

SWEET LITTLE KATE.

Mr. Tatham describes Kate Kelly as "a dear, sweet little girl, with dark hair." Kate was shortly built, measuring about four feet six. "I agree with Mr. Barrett that she was never 'the daring Kate' so often described, affirms our historian. "She was too sweet and gentle for that."

JIMMY DONS THE ARMOR.

One day in the courthouse the police asked Jimmy if he would care to don Ned Kelly's suit of armor, which had been taken from him. Jimmy readily assented, and here is how he described the experience : — I tried to look through the eye slit with my head held in the ordinary position the slit would close, but if I tilted my head backwards a little it gradually opened to about an inch and I could see quite well. The body piece was put together very roughly. In the front a small piece of metal was welded on below the trunk, ex-tending to just below the knees. I think the armor was made out of of thin, worn-out plow shares. It did not fit, and I was glad to get out of it.

THE BYRNE FAMILY.

"The Byrnes were a very decent family", Mr. Tatham concluded. "I saw Byrne's sister confirmed in the Beechworth Catholic Church. She was employed by Mrs. Fealy, of Black Springs."

THE AFTERMATH.

Since the "days of '49" Mr. Tatham was married, in Geelong, and after some years spent in Kew he and Mrs. Tatham came to Healesville, where they have been well known and highly respected residents for many years. They have a grown-up family of five, two boys and three girls. Mr. Tatham obviously loves to recall the stirring happenings of the early pioneering days — when he was "Young Jimmy" and the world was wide.

Beechworth Police Court

ASSAULT.—Robert Woods, a rather inoffensive-looking man, was charged with having assaulted Ah Nam, who appeared in court with his head bandaged up. Elizabeth Salsbury, a girl of fifteen or sixteen years of age, residing at Sebastopol, said that on Friday evening she was with defendant, who was driving his wagon on the Woolshed-road; her brother and sister were with her; after having gone about a mile and a half, defendant missed a piece of iron from the saddle; they all went back to look for it, and found it lying on the road; after they had found the piece of iron, they all sat down on the road-side; when sitting there a Chinaman came out of the bushes, said something to Bob in Chinese, and then struck him with his fist and afterwards with a slipper; Bob struck him with the piece of iron produced, and then ran away; the Chinaman broke a stick and ran after him. In answer to defendant, witness said that she heard the Chinaman say he would kill him. Ellen Salsbury, a younger sister, corroborated the evidence of the previous witness. Joseph Burns, a laborer, said that on Friday evening he met the complainant, Ah Nam, and with him proceeded towards the Woolshed; on their way they overtook defendant and the previous witnesses; some words passed between them, when the Chinaman took off his slipper and struck defendant about the head; he struck him several times, and defendant hit him back with the piece of iron he had in his hand; the Chinaman procured a sapling, and defendant ran away. In answer to defendant, witness said that he did not hear the Chinaman say he would kill him; defendant said to him to take the Chinaman away, as he did not want to strike him. Dr Mousse gave evidence as to the nature of the wounds received by defendant; neither of them was of a dangerous character, and from the instrument used it was probable that one blow had caused them both. Ah Nam, who appeared like the man who had won the fight, said that he went after the girls to ask them to come and look after the place, when defendant interfered and struck him with a piece of iron; he had not struck the defendant first. The bench said there was no doubt the defendant had received considerable provocation, but not sufficient to justify him in using such a weapon as that produced. Fined 40s, with the alternative of fourteen days' imprisonment.

Source: Ovens and Murray Advertiser

(Beechworth, Vic. : 1855 - 1918),

Tuesday 8 April 1873, page 2

Fire at the Chinese Camp

FIRE AT THE BEECHWORTH CHINESE CAMP.

Lin Tin believes that where there is smoke there must be fire. He finds he is right, but scorns the help of Joss. The fire caused by a gossiping European woman.

Some few minutes before one o'clock yesterday, Lin Tin, a dweller in the Chinese Camp, observed smoke in unusual quantities issuing from the residence of Ah Chee, one of a group of huts that nestled together in accordance with Asiatic fashion, at the eastern side of the camp. Lin Tin thought where there was so much smoke there must be flame, and proceeded to the dwelling of Ah Chee, to discover that it was on fire. He did not wait to call on Joss, but tried his best to put the fire out, unfortunately without success; the building was old, dry and inflammable, and the rapid progress of the flames bewildered Lin Tin, and some few seconds elapsed before he could call for assistance. Soon, however, the cry of "fire, fire," or it's equivalent in Chinese, resounded through the camp, and, like bees when their hive is disturbed, the Chinamen swarmed from out the neighboring stores and huts. A few years' residence in the colony has not been without its effect in removing the passiveness that used to be exhibited by the Celestials when fires broke out in or near their dwellings; they did not stand with arms folded, but got hold of buckets, and, in somewhat disorderly fashion, tried to arrest the progress of the flames by means of water from a race at the rear of the burning buildings. By this time the smoke had commenced to ascend in dense volumes, so as to be visible in Beechworth. The fire-bell was rung, and the alarm raised in the town and numbers of people set out on horseback, on foot, and in vehicles, for the camp. Amongst the first on the ground were the police, under the command of Sergeant Baber, who rendered excellent service in organising the Chinese, and directing their efforts to one common spot. It was seen that it would be useless to attempt to save the group of huts that were crowded together, but a small garden adjoining Nam Sing's residence made a kind of gap between the burning buildings and the rest of the camp, and all efforts were concentrated towards preventing the flames from passing that gap. What little wind there was fortunately seconded the exertions of the Europeans and the Chinese, who worked might and main to arrest the progress of the fire. But for this fact nothing could have possibly saved the camp from destruction. As it was, some twelve dwellinghouses and one lottery shop were burned to the ground. Commencing in Ah Chee's house, facing the Stanley road, the flames spread to the right and left, first one and then another of the little dens in which the Chinese love to dwell igniting. Next to Ah Chee's house was a lottery shop; that speedily went, and for some time it was feared that a man had lost his life, but the missing man, Ah Cheong, turned up before the fire had been entirely subdued. Adjoining the lottery shop were the houses of Nam Sing, Te Lin, Ah Tak, Ah Gee, Ah Ho, Yu Men, and others, all of which were burned to the ground. A jeweller's shop, adjoining the private residence of Nam Sing, belonging to Ah Fan, was pulled down by the Chinamen, a number of whom worked well in keeping the boards and the roof of the store beyond tolerably moist, and thus preventing them from igniting. Several of the Europeans, resident in the neighborhood, notably Mr. Strugnell, did yeoman's service, and to the exertions of both Europeans and Chinamen it is attributable that the loss of property was not considerably greater. Considering the inflammable nature of the buildings of which the camp is composed, it is really wonderful that the whole of the buildings were not destroyed. As matters stand, although damage has been done to the extent of some £500 or £600, yet the loss is much less than had the fire occurred in any other portion of the camp; only private houses were destroyed, the stores and principal buildings escaping without damage. During the afternoon, while efforts were being made to quench the embers of the burned buildings, a Chinaman named Ah Mi sustained some rather severe burns on the neck and chest; his injuries, however, are not of a dangerous character. The fire is believed to have been caused by the carelessness of Ah Chee's housekeeper, a European woman, who left a fire burning on the hearth while she proceeded to enjoy a gossip with some of her neighbors.-

—O. and M. Advertiser.

Source: Herald (Melbourne, Vic.: 1861 - 1954),

Thursday 20 March 1873, page 3

The Spring Creek Chinese Camp, Beechworth, circa 1870s, as Joe Byrne and Ah Nam would have seen it.

Courtesy: Burke Museum, Beechworth

James Ingram's bookshop, Camp Street, Beechworth, circa early 1870s.

Courtesy: Burke Museum, Beechworth

It's not hard to see this young gent as a pre-outlawry Joe Byrne, especially when compared to the only verified studio portrait of Joe.
[Courtesy: Burke Museum, Beechworth]

Ingram's bookshop as it appears today.

[Author's collection]

Ah Nam's mark (top) and James Ingram's signature (bottom) from the documents of the inquest into Ellen Doyle's death.

[Courtesy: Public Records Office Victoria, VPRS 24/P0000]

Sebastopol Flat as it appears now. It is hard to imagine this was once a thriving mining village.
Author's Collection

Interior of the Burke Museum with the famous Maltby world globe under the archway.
Author's collection

The famous stained glass window above the taxidermy display in the Burke Museum

Photographer: Aidan Phelan

Bird's-eye view of Beechworth looking towards Mayday Hills Asylum, circa 1880. The Chinese Camp would have been at the left of the photograph.
Author's collection

Beechworth, looking down Ford Street towards the gaol, circa 1920.
Author's collection

Opening Of The Railway To Beechworth.- View Of The Township And Terminus. The Illustrated Australian News, November 1, 1876.
Courtesy: State Library Victoria [IAN01/11/76/169]

Notes

Prologue:

- Ah Nam being a miner and residing in the Sebastopol Chinese Camp. (*Ovens and Murray Advertiser*, November 17, 1877.)
- Ettie Noble residing with Sarah Payne. *(Ovens and Murray Advertiser, July 31, 1883.)*
- Ah Fee being married to Elizabeth Ah Fee. (*Ovens and Murray Advertiser, May 20, 1880.*)
- Sarah Payne running a brothel. (*Ovens and Murray Advertiser*, September 22, 1877.)
- Ettie Noble working as a prostitute. (*Ovens and Murray Advertiser, December 11, 1883.*)
- Thomas Lloyd obtaining the licence for the Eagle Hotel in the Woolshed Valley. (*Ovens and Murray Advertiser*, July 14, 1857)
- Nam Shing owning the Sun Quong Goon Hotel. (*Ovens and Murray Advertiser*, December 16, 1879.)

Narrative:

- Margaret Byrne running a dairy. (*Ovens and Murray Advertiser*, July 29, 1879) and (*The Fatal Friendship*, 2003, p.20)
- Crawford and Co's Coach travelling from Beechworth to El Dorado. (*Ovens and Murray Advertiser*, April 19, 1873.)
- Letter to the editor complaining of inadequate signposts in the Woolshed Valley. (*Ovens and Murray Advertiser*, March 18, 1873.)
- Dunlop's Scotch Pie Shop in Camp Street. (Ovens and Murray Advertiser, August 28, 1875.)

- James Wallace being the school friend of Joe Byrne and Aaron Sherritt. (*The Age*, June 10, 1883.)
- Daniel McNamara's saddlery in Ford Street. (*Ovens and Murray Advertiser*, August 28, 1875.)
- James Tatham being the friend of Joe Byrne and Aaron Sherritt. (*Healesville and Yarra Glen Guardian*, June 16, 1934.)
- James Tatham being employed by Beechworth grocer William Greer. (*Healesville and Yarra Glen Guardian*, June 16, 1934.)
- John Carew's bootmaker's shop in Ford Street. (*Ovens and Murray Advertiser*, February 7, 1874.)
- Joe Byrne visiting James Ingram's bookshop in Camp Street. (The Fatal Friendship, 2003, p.24.)
- Fire in the Chinese Camp and Ah Chee working as wood carter. (*Ovens and Murray Advertiser*, September 17, 1868.)
- James Ingram being gifted a jar of preserved ginger, after defending the Chinese from the attacks of young Europeans. (*Ovens and Murray Advertiser*, May 19, 1881.)
- Nam Shing being acquainted with Joe Byrne. (*The Fatal Friendship*, 2003, p.24.)
- Joe Byrne being called 'Ah Joe'. (*Royal Commission*, q.14973, p.542.)
- Ah Fook sharing a gold claim with Aaron and Jack Sherritt. (*The Fatal Friendship*, 2003, p.24.)
- Aaron Sherritt working with Beechworth pound keeper John Phelan. (*The Fatal Friendship*, 2003, p.30.)
- Joe Byrne and Aaron stealing fruit from Antonio Wick's orchard in Sebastopol. (*The Fatal Friendship*, 2003, p.16.)
- The Vine Hotel being located along Sydney Road. (*Ovens and Murray Advertiser*, May 16, 1867.)
- The Vine Hotel's orchard. (*Ovens and Murray Advertiser*, January 30, 1875.)
- The fight between Ah Nam and Robert Woods. (*Ovens and Murray Advertiser*, April 8, 1873.)
- James and Elizabeth Salisbury being called to give evidence alongside Joe Byrne at the inquest and trial for the murder of Ah Suey. (*Ovens and Murray Advertiser*, May 10, 1872) and (*Ovens and Murray Advertiser*, October 18, 1872.)
- Israel Abraham owning a store in Sebastopol. (*Background to Beechworth*, 1994, p.60.)
- Giles Thrower being a Sebastopol Blacksmith.

(*Background to Beechworth*, 1994, p.60.)

- James Salisbury residing at Sebastopol. (*Ovens and Murray Advertiser*, October 18, 1872) and (*Ovens and Murray Advertiser*, July 29, 1879.)
- Ah Nam receiving medical care at the Ovens District Hospital following the fight with Robert Woods and being referred to as 'Broken China'. (*Ovens and Murray Advertiser*, April 7, 1873.)

The Author

Georgina Stones was born and raised in Tasmania, but has recently made the move across Bass Strait to reside in Victoria. She has a love of history, with the lives of Australian outlaws Joe Byrne and Michael Howe her main interests in that field.

She attended school in Ulverstone and has since studied journalism through Deakin University. Her natural inquisitiveness and perseverance have paid off in her work on *An Outlaw's Journal*, uncovering many previously forgotten or overlooked aspects of the life of Joe Byrne, particularly in regards to his early life and connections to the Chinese community. She also researches and writes for her website *Michael Howe: Governor of the Woods* for which she has been interviewed on ABC Radio and featured in *Traces* magazine.

The Illustrator

Aidan Phelan is the writer and historian for *A Guide to Australian Bushranging*, which has been bringing Australia's outlaw heritage to a worldwide audience since 2017. In 2021 he was featured in a series of interviews on ABC Radio Hobart and Northern Tasmania discussing the history of bushrangers in Tasmania, and was interviewed for *The Hobart Magazine* about bushranger "Rocky" Whelan.

He has also worked as an illustrator, contributing work for Judy Lawson's *The Clarke Bushrangers: A Clash of Cultures* in 2020, and regularly provides illustrations for *An Outlaw's Journal* by Georgina Stones.

In 2020 he self-published his first novel, *Glenrowan*, which dramatised the final months of the Kelly Outbreak. He is also developing *Glenrowan* as a television miniseries with filmmaker Matthew Holmes (*The Legend of Ben Hall*).

The Outlaw

Joseph Byrne was born to Irish parents in Victoria, Australia, around 1856/57. His father died when Joe was just a boy and he soon looked for work around the Woolshed Valley, where he lived. He spent much of his time with the Chinese in Sebastopol and Beechworth, and with his best friend Aaron Sherritt.

In his early twenties, Joe joined Aaron and Ned Kelly in a horse stealing operation, before being implicated in the police murders at Stringybark Creek in 1878, alongside Ned Kelly, Dan Kelly and Steve Hart. Joe was outlawed, eventually gaining a reward for his capture of £2000. He was an accomplice in two bank robberies and after being coerced into murdering Aaron, was killed during a siege at Glenrowan on 26 June 1880. He is buried in Benalla cemetery.

www.ingramcontent.com/pod-product-compliance
Lightning Source LLC
Chambersburg PA
CBHW060756310726
48980CB00002B/114
* 9 7 8 0 6 4 5 3 7 8 4 0 5 *